Having a baby—Jake's baby—made life too impossible.

"Is something wrong, Amy?" Her glazed eyes cleared enough to see he was observing her very keenly.

Would their child have his eyes?

Her stomach cramped.

"No," she forced out. "Everything's fine." *Except I'm probably pregnant.*

Initially a French/English teacher, EMMA DARCY changed careers to computer programming before marriage and motherhood settled her into a community life. Creative urges were channeled into oil painting, pottery, designing and overseeing the construction and decoration of two homes, all in the midst of keeping up with three lively sons and the very social life of her businessman husband, Frank. Very much a people person and always interested in relationships, she finds the world of romance fiction a happy one and the challenge of creating her own cast of characters very addictive. She enjoys traveling, and her experiences often find their way into her books. Emma Darcy lives on a country property in New South Wales, Australia.

Books by Emma Darcy

Don't miss any of our special offers. Write to us at the following address for information on our newest releases.

Harlequin Reader Service
U.S.: 3010 Walden Ave., P.O. Box 1325, Buffalo, NY 14269
Canadian: P.O. Box 609, Fort Erie, Ont. L2A 5X3

EMMA DARCY

The Marriage Decider

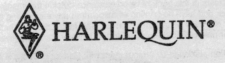

TORONTO • NEW YORK • LONDON
AMSTERDAM • PARIS • SYDNEY • HAMBURG
STOCKHOLM • ATHENS • TOKYO • MILAN • MADRID
PRAGUE • WARSAW • BUDAPEST • AUCKLAND

ISBN 0-373-12020-6

THE MARRIAGE DECIDER

First North American Publication 1999.

CHAPTER ONE

IS YOUR MAN ABOUT TO DUMP YOU?
SPOTTING THE EXIT SIGNS

THE headline teaser on the glossy cover of her favourite magazine caused a roll of nausea through Amy Taylor's stomach. It was the new December issue, out today, and the advice it contained was too late to be of any help. A pity the article hadn't been written months ago. She might have recognised what had been going on with Steve, at least been somewhat prepared for the bombshell that had hit her over the weekend.

Though that was doubtful. She wouldn't have applied the exit signs to her relationship with Steve. Although neither of them had pushed for marriage—free spirits should never shackle themselves, he had insisted—after *five* years together—a mini-marriage in anyone's book—continuity had become a state of mind. She'd been hopelessly blind to what was really happening.

Free spirits! Amy gnashed her teeth over that remembered phrase. There was nothing free-spirited about rushing headlong into marriage with someone else! The blonde he'd bedded behind Amy's back, was shackling Steve with an ease that was painfully insulting. With the result that Amy was certainly being left *free!* Though hardly free-spirited.

Here she was, comprehensively dumped, twenty-eight years old, single again, and suffering the worst case of

Monday blues she could ever remember having. It was sheer masochism to pick up the new issue of the magazine with *that* article in it—a clear case of punishing herself—but maybe she needed to have all the signs spelled out so she'd know better next time. *If* there ever was a next time.

At her age, the market for unattached men was slim, especially men worth having. Amy brooded over that depressing fact as she paid the news vendor for the magazine and walked down Alfred Street to her workplace, the last office building facing the harbour on Milsons Point, a highly privileged piece of real estate which she was in no mood to appreciate this morning.

Ahead of her, summer sunshine had turned Sydney Harbour into a glittering expanse of blue, patterned harmoniously by boats and ferries carving white wakes across it. To her left, Bradfield Park offered the peaceful green of newly mown lawns, invitingly shadowed by the great Coat-hanger bridge that dominated the skyline, feeding the city with an endless stream of commuter traffic. Amy was totally oblivious to all of it. For her, there was only the dark gloom of her thoughts.

Dumped for a blonde, a smart, pregnant blonde. Nobody got pregnant by accident these days. Not at thirty-two. Amy was sure it had been a calculated gamble, the hook to pull Steve in and tie him up for better or for worse. And it had worked. The wedding date was already set. One month from today. New Year's Eve. Happy New Year, Amy thought bitterly, seeing a long stretch of loneliness for herself.

Maybe at thirty-two, she'd feel desperate enough to snitch someone else's man. After all, if he was willing, as Steve must have been…but how could you ever really trust a man who cheated on the woman he was living with? Amy wrinkled her nose. She'd be better off on her own.

But she didn't feel better off. She felt sick, empty, lost in a world that had suddenly turned unfamiliar, hostile, her bearings torn away. Tears filled her eyes as she pushed open the door to her workplace and barged into the foyer, needing the safe mooring of her job to fight the flood of misery she could barely contain.

"Hi! Boss in?" she aimed at Kate Bradley, her vision too embarrassingly blurred to meet the receptionist's eyes directly. Besides, Kate was a gorgeous blonde, a typical choice for Jake Carter's front desk woman, and another reminder of pain for her right now.

"Not yet," came the cheerful reply. "Something must have held him up."

Jake was an early bird, invariably in his office ahead of Amy. She was intensely relieved to hear he was late this morning, giving her time to get herself together before those yellow wolf eyes of his noted anything amiss.

She certainly didn't need the humiliation of having to explain why her mascara was running, which it probably was from her furious blinking. Moisture had to be clinging to her lashes. She pressed the elevator button, willing the doors to open instantly.

"Have a good weekend?" Kate asked, addressing Amy's back, blithely unaware of any problem.

Amy half turned, not wishing to appear totally rude. "No. It was the pits," she blurted out, giving vent to some of her pent-up emotion.

"Oh! Guess things can only get better," Kate offered sympathetically.

"I wish," Amy muttered.

The elevator doors obligingly opened. The ride up to the floor she shared with Jake was mercifully brief and she headed straight for the washroom to effect repairs. Once safely enclosed in privacy she tore tissues from the box on the vanity bench and began wiping away the smeared make-up around her eyes.

She couldn't afford to look as though she was falling apart. As Jake Carter's personal assistant, she had to stay on top of everything, as well as maintain the class image of the company. *Wide Blue Yonder Pty Ltd.* sold its services to the mega-rich who had no tolerance for bungling. Perfection was expected and perfection had to be delivered. Jake had drummed that into her from day one.

Two years she'd been working with him and she knew him through and through. Nothing escaped his notice and she needed cast-iron armour to stop him from getting under her skin. He was a brilliant salesman, a masterly entrepreneur, a stickler for detail, and a dyed-in-the-wool womaniser.

He was certainly single, and frequently unattached, but the chance of forging anything but a brief physical affair with him was nil. She couldn't help fancying him now and then—no woman alive wouldn't—but Amy had too much self-esteem to ever allow herself to be used for fun. Casual intimacy did not appeal to her.

Jake was into *experiences* with women, not relationships, the more exciting and varied the better. To Amy's accumulated knowledge, he had a low threshold of interest in any woman. They came and went with such regularity, she lost track of their names.

Though they did have one thing in common. They were all stunning to look at and made no secret of their availability to answer any need Jake Carter might have for them. He didn't have to chase. He simply had to choose.

Jake the rake, Amy had privately christened him. As far as she could see, he never scratched more than the surface of those who rolled through his life. Amy had figured very early on that keeping an impervious surface to Jake Carter was a prime requirement for keeping her job. Let other women fall victim to his animal magnetism. She had Steve.

Except she didn't anymore.

Tears welled again.

She stared at the soggy mess of herself in the mirror, battling the sense of defeat that was swamping her. Maybe she should dye her hair blonde. The ridiculous thought almost made her laugh. Her emphatically arched eyebrows and the double rows of lashes were uncompromisingly black, her eyes such a dark blue they were almost violet. She'd look stupid as anything other than a brunette.

Besides, she liked her hair. It was thick and glossy and the feathery razor cut around her face gave the shoulder-length bob a soft frame for her rather angular features. She didn't mind them, either. The high slant of her cheekbones balanced her squarish jawline and although her mouth was on the wide side, it did not look disproportionate. It more or less complemented the slight flare of her nostrils and the full curve of her lips was decidedly feminine. Her nose was straight, her neck was long enough to wear any jewellery well and her figure was fine, curvy enough in the right places and slim enough to carry off the clothes she liked.

There was nothing wrong with her looks, Amy fiercely asserted to herself. Jake Carter wouldn't have hired her if he'd found her wanting in that department. His clients expected glamour. After all, they bought or chartered luxury yachts and jet planes. *Wide Blue Yonder* catered to their every whim, and charged them the earth for it. Jake insisted that his staff be as pleasing to the eye as everything else connected to his business. Image, he preached, was every bit as important as supplying what was demanded.

Though Amy had little doubt he was pleasing himself as much as anyone else. He made no secret of enjoying the visual pleasure of his female work force. He might call it *class,* but he was such a sexy beast, Amy was certain he revelled in exercising his right to choose a stimulating environment for himself.

She took several deep, calming breaths, opened her handbag, fished out her emergency make-up kit, and set to work, creating an unblemished facade to present to her boss. His lateness this morning was a stroke of luck. She couldn't bank on any more luck running her way. Somehow she had to shut Steve and his pregnant wife-to-be out of her mind and concentrate on performing every task Jake handed her with her usual efficiency. It was the only way to avoid drawing unwelcome attention.

Satisfied she looked as good as she could in the circumstances, Amy returned her make-up kit to her handbag. Having washed and dried her hands, she smoothed the skirt of her scarlet linen shift over her hips, wishing linen didn't crease quite so much. But it was *in* this season, despite its crushability, and the bright colour was a much-needed spirit-booster. At least, that was what she'd argued as she'd donned it this morning.

Pride had insisted the expensive dress should not be wasted. She'd bought it last week, planning to wear it to Steve's office Christmas party. Now she saw it as a too belligerent statement that she would not mourn for him, a pathetic statement, given the heartsickness she was trying to hide. Still, it was too late to change her mind about it now and it might distract Jake Carter from picking up on her inner distress.

The tension of having to face him eased when she discovered his office empty and there was no sign of his having arrived for work. Puzzled as she was by his uncharacteristic lateness, Amy was nevertheless relieved to have the extra time to establish an air of busy occupation.

She settled at her desk and slipped the magazine she'd bought into the bottom drawer, out of sight and hopefully out of mind until she could read it in private. Concentration on her job was top priority now. She turned on her computer, connected to the Internet and brought up the E-mail that had come in over the weekend.

She was printing it out for Jake's perusal when she heard the telltale whoosh of the elevator doors opening to the corridor which ran adjacent to their offices. Her nerves tightened. Her mind raced through defensive tactics.

Jake would probably drop into her office to explain

his lateness, then use the connecting door to enter his own. After a perfunctory greeting she could plunge straight into discussing the mail with him. It contained a number of queries to be answered. The sooner they got down to business, the better.

Jake had a habit of throwing personal inquiries at her on Monday mornings and she desperately wanted to avoid them today. This past weekend didn't bear thinking about let alone commenting upon. Not to Jake Carter.

If there was one thing more difficult to deflect than his sizzling sex appeal, it was his curiosity. Give him even a hint of an opening and he'd capitilise on it, probing for more information every which way. The man had a mind as sharp as a razor.

The door to her office rattled as it was thrust open. Amy's heart kicked in trepidation. She kept her gaze fastened on the printer as she steeled herself not to reveal even the tiniest crack of vulnerability to the dangerous impact of her boss's strong charisma.

In her mind's eye she ticked off what she had to meet with perfect equanimity; the tall, muscle-packed physique exuding male power, skin so uniformly tanned it seemed to gleam with the warm kiss of sunshine, a face full of charm, a slight smile accentuating the sensuality of a mouth that somehow combined strength and teasing whimsy, an inviting twinkle in eyes all the more fascinating for their drooping lids, causing them to look triangular in shape, accentuating the intensity of the intelligence burning through the intriguing amber irises. Last, but not least, was an enticing wealth of dark, wavy hair, threaded with silver, giving him an air of maturity that encouraged trust in his judgement, though Amy knew him to be only thirty-four.

She suspected he'd look no different in ten or even twenty years' time. He'd still be making every woman's heart flutter. It was a power she resented, given his fickleness, and she clung to that resentment as she looked up from the print-out to give the necessary acknowledgement of his presence.

Her gaze caught on the capsule he was carrying.

Shock wiped out her own concerns.

Jake the rake with a baby?

A baby?

Steve's pleas for understanding pounded through her mind...responsibility, commitment, the rights of the child, being a full-time father...

Jake the rake in that role?

Amy lost all her moorings. She was hopelessly adrift.

"You don't think fatherhood becomes me?"

The amused lilt of his sexy, purring voice jerked her gaze up. He chuckled at her confounded expression as he strolled forward and plonked the capsule on her desk.

"Cute little tyke, isn't he?"

Amy rolled back her chair and stood up, staring down at what looked like a very small baby who was blessedly fast asleep. Only its head and a tiny clenched hand were visible above the bunny rug tucked snugly around the mound of its body. How old it was Amy couldn't guess, but she didn't think it was newborn.

"This...is yours?" Her voice came out like a strangled squawk, disbelief choking more than her mind.

He grinned, enjoying having provoked her obvious

loss of composure. "More or less," he answered, his eyes agleam with wicked mischief.

She belatedly registered the teasing. Resentment flared out of her control, fuelled by the pain of having to accept Steve's full-on commitment to fatherhood with a woman other than herself.

"Congratulations!" She arched her eyebrows higher. "I take it the mother is happy with this more or less arrangement?"

"Uh-oh!" He wagged a finger at her, his sparkling amusement scraping her nerves raw. "Your bad opinion of me is showing, Amy. And it's absolutely undeserved."

Like hell it was! She hastily constructed a deadpan look to frustrate him. "I do apologise. Your personal affairs are, of course, none of my business."

"Joshua's mother trusts me implicitly," he declared loftily.

"How nice!"

"She knows I can be counted upon in an emergency."

"Yes. You always do rise to an occasion."

He laughed at the dry irony in her voice. "I see you've recovered. But I did have you lost for a word earlier on," he said triumphantly.

"Would you like me to be speechless more often?"

"What fun would the game be then?" Sheer devilment in his eyes.

Amy deliberately remained silent.

He heaved a sigh. "Determined to frustrate me." He shook his head at her. "Challenge is the spice of life to me, Amy."

She ignored the comment, giving him nothing to feed off.

"Okay," he conceded. "Joshua's mum is my sister, Ruth. Everything fell in on her this morning. My brother-in-law dislocated his shoulder, playing squash. She had to take him to hospital. I was elected as emergency baby-sitter so I got landed with my nephew for the duration. Ruth will come by here to pick him up when she can."

Light dawned. "You're the baby's uncle."

"And his godfather." The teasing grin came back. "You see before you a staunch family man."

From the safe distance of being once removed, Amy thought cynically.

"I'll just pop him down here." He lifted the capsule off her desk and placed it on the floor beside the filing cabinets. "Great little sleeper. Went off in the car and hasn't budged since."

He was leaving the baby with her!

Amy stared at the tiny bundle of humanity—the result of intimacy between a man and a woman—a bond of life that went on and on, no matter what the parents chose to do—a link that couldn't be broken—a baby.

Her whole body clenched against the anguish flooding through her. For this Steve had left her. For this Steve was marrying another woman. Their years together meant nothing...compared to this. He'd covered up his infidelity. Amy hadn't even suspected it. It was the baby who had ended their five-year-long relationship...the baby the man-trap blonde was having...part of Steve he couldn't let go.

And Amy couldn't blame him for that, however deeply it pained her.

A baby deserved to have its father.

But the betrayal of all they'd shared together hurt so much, so terribly much...

"This today's mail?"

She hadn't been aware of Jake backtracking to her desk. The question swung her head towards him. He'd picked up the sheets from the printer. "Yes," she answered numbly.

"I'll take it into my office." He made a beeline for the connecting door, waving at the capsule as he went. "There's a bottle of formula and a couple of disposable nappies in that bag at Joshua's feet. Shouldn't be a problem."

So arrogantly casual, dumping his responsibility for the baby onto her!

Resentment started to burn again.

He opened the door and paused, looking back, oh so sleekly elegant in his grey silk suit, unruffled, uncreased, supremely self-assured, the tantalising little smile quirking his mouth.

"By the way, you look utterly stunning in red, Amy. You should wear it more often."

He winked flirtatiously at her and was gone, the door closing smoothly behind him.

Amy saw red.

Her mind was a haze of red.

Her heart pumped red-hot blood through her veins.

Her brain sizzled. All of her sizzled.

Since Jake Carter enjoyed cracking her composure, he could damned well enjoy a monumental crack! She was *not* going to look after someone else's baby…a baby who had no connection to her whatsoever. It wasn't her job. And today of all days, she didn't need a vivid reminder of what she had lost and why. Let Jake Carter look after his own…the staunch family man! The Godfather!

She looked down at the baby, still peacefully asleep, oblivious to the turbulent emotions it stirred in Amy. She looked at the plastic bag at the foot of the capsule. It was printed with fun Disney characters. Today, Jake Carter could have *fun* with his nephew. The game with her was over and she didn't care if he fired her for it. In fact, if he dared to try any pressure on her over minding his nephew she'd get in first and dump him.

It would probably be a new experience for him, getting dumped by a woman. And he wouldn't be expecting it, either. There hadn't been any exit signs for him to spot.

A savage little smile curled her lips.

She was about to give Jake Carter a red letter day.

And serve him right, too!

CHAPTER TWO

AMY barged into her boss's office, wishing the capsule swinging in her hand was a cudgel to beat him with. It infuriated her further to find him leaning back in his executive chair, feet up on his executive desk, hands cupping the back of his head, gazing smugly at the panoramic harbour view through his executive windows.

No work was being done. The mail she had printed out for him had been tossed on the in-tray. He looked as if he was revelling in recalling the pleasures he had undoubtedly indulged in over the weekend. While she had been dealt one killing blow after another.

It wasn't fair!

Nothing was fair!

But by God! She'd make *this man* honour his commitment!

Her unheralded entrance drew a bland look of inquiry. "Some problem?"

Welcome to hell on wheels! she thought, marching straight up to his desk and heaving the capsule onto it. She did refrain from knocking his feet off. She didn't want to wake the baby. It wasn't the infant's fault that his uncle was a male chauvinist pig.

With her hands free, she planted them on her hips and took her stance. Apparently fascinated by the vision of his normally cool personal assistant on the warpath, Jake stayed locked where he was, which suited Amy just fine. She opened fire at point-blank range.

"This baby...is your responsibility."

Her voice shook, giving it a huskiness that robbed it of the authority needed. She hastily worked some moisture into her mouth and resumed speaking with more strength.

"Your sister elected *you* to be her son's baby-sitter."

She stretched her mouth into a smile designed to turn Medusa to stone. It must have worked because he still didn't move. Or speak.

"She trusts you implicitly," Amy said sweetly. "As she should since you're his godfather. And a staunch family man."

It gave her a fierce pleasure to throw that claim back in his face, an even fiercer pleasure to see him look so stunned and at a loss for a ready reply. Join the club, brother, she thought, and fired the last volley.

"Looking after your nephew is not my job. Hire someone who specialises in baby-sitting if you can't do it yourself. In the meantime, he belongs with you."

She swivelled on her heel and headed for the door, her spine stiff, her shoulders squared, her head tilted high. If Jake Carter so much as breathed at her she would wheel and attack him again.

There wasn't a sound.

Silence followed her to the door.

She didn't look back.

She made her exit on a wave of righteous fervour.

It wasn't until the door was shut and she was alone in her own office, that the silence she'd left behind her took on an ominous quality in her mind.

Silence…

Like the silence after Steve had walked out.

She'd lost her man.

Amy closed her eyes as the realisation of what she'd done rushed in on her.

She was about to lose her job.

Lose everything.

This black day had just turned blacker.

CHAPTER THREE

AMY lost track of time. She found herself sitting at her desk and didn't remember sinking into her chair. It was as though she'd pressed a self-destruct button and her whole world had slipped out of control, shattering around her.

Vengeance...that's what she'd wreaked on Jake Carter...paying him out for what Steve had done to her. And she'd had no right to do it. No right at all.

A personal assistant was supposed to personally assist. That was what she was paid for. Any other day she wouldn't have blinked an eyelid at being left with a baby to mind. She would have taken it in her stride without so much as a murmur of protest, cynically accepting that Jake, the rake, wouldn't want to be bothered by a baby. Besides which, in business hours, his time was more important than hers. He was the one who pulled in the profits.

She slumped forward, propped her elbows on the desk and dropped her head into her hands. Dear merciful God! Was there some way out of the hole she'd dug for herself?

She couldn't afford to walk away from this job, not now she was alone. Steve's departure meant the rent on the apartment would double for her unless she got someone else in to share the cost. These few weeks before Christmas was not a good time for changes.

Besides, who would pay her as much as Jake did? Her salary was more than generous for her qualifications. And she would miss the perks that came with meeting and doing business for rich and famous people.

Her gaze lifted and ruefully skirted the photographs hanging on the walls; celebrities on their luxury yachts, on board their private jets, travelling in style to exciting places, wining and dining in classy surroundings, perfect service on tap.

Of course Jake was in all the photographs, showing off his clientele and what he had provided for them. The man was a brilliant salesman. The photographs were public proof that he was the one to deliver what was desired.

And the plain truth was, however much he provoked her with his teasing and wicked ways, Amy did, for the most part, enjoy the challenge of matching wits with him. He kept her on her toes, goaded her into performing at her best, and the work was never boring. Neither was he.

She'd miss him.

Badly.

Especially with Steve gone.

She'd miss this plush office, too.

Where else would she get a workplace that could even come near to matching what she had here at *Wide Blue Yonder?*

Her gaze drifted around, picking up on all she could be about to lose. The carpet was the jewel-like turquoise colour of coral reef lagoons, the paintwork the mellow yellow shade of sandy beaches, outlined in glossy white. Fresh arrangements of tropical flowers were brought in every week, exotic blooms in orange and scarlet mixed with glowing greenery. Every modern technological aid for business was at her fingertips—no expense spared in providing her with the best of everything.

Then there was the million dollar view—an extension of the vista that could be seen from Jake's office—Darling Harbour and Balmain directly across the water, Goat Island, and stretching along this shoreline, Luna Park with its cluster of carnival rides and entertainment booths.

Mortified at her own lunacy for giving none of this a thought before barging in to confront Jake, Amy pushed out of her chair and moved over to the picture window overlooking the grinning clown face that marked the entrance to the old amusement park. Fun, it promised. Just like Jake. Except she'd hot-headedly wiped fun off today's agenda.

She should go back into his office and apologise.

But how to explain her behaviour?

Never had she struck such a blistering attitude with him. He was probably sitting in there, mulling over what it meant, and he wouldn't gloss over it. Not Jake Carter. No way would he leave it alone. If he wasn't thinking of firing her for insubordination, he was plotting how to use her outburst to his advantage.

She shivered.

Give Jake even a molehill of an advantage and he could build it into a mountain that put him on top of any game he wanted to play. She'd seen him do it over and over again. If he let her stay on...

The sound of the door between their offices being opened froze her train of thought. It raised prickles around the nape of her neck. Panic screamed along her nerves and cramped her heart. She'd left it too late to take some saving initiative. In helpless anguish she turned to face the man who held her immediate future in his hands.

He stood in the doorway, commanding her attention by the sheer force of his presence. The absence of any hint of a smile was stomach-wrenching. He observed her in silence for several tension-riven seconds, his eyes focused intensely on hers. Amy's mind screamed at her to say something, offer an olive branch, anything to smooth over what she'd done, but she couldn't tear her tongue off the roof of her mouth.

"I'm sorry."

Soft words...words she should have said. She stared at his mouth. Had they really come from him or had she imagined it? Yet how could she imagine an apology when she hadn't expected it?

His lips twisted into a rueful grimace. "I was out of line, dumping Joshua on you and taking it for granted you'd mind him for me."

Incredulity held her tongue-tied.

The grimace tilted up into an appealing smile. "Guess I thought all women melted over babies. I didn't see it as an imposition. More like a novelty."

She felt hopelessly screwed up. Her hand shot out in an agitated gesture. "I...over-reacted," she managed, her voice a bare croak.

He shrugged. "Hell, what do I know? You're so buttoned up about your private life. There must be some reason you're not married to the guy you've been living with all these years." His eyebrows slanted in an expression of caring concern. "Is there a problem about having a baby?"

The sympathetic tone did it.

Like the trumpets that brought down the walls of Jericho, it struck chords in Amy that triggered a collapse of her defences. Tears welled into her eyes and she couldn't find the will to stop them. She wanted to say it wasn't her fault but the lump in her throat was impassable.

She had a blurry glimpse of shock on Jake Carter's face, then he was moving, looming towards her, and the next thing she knew his arms had enveloped her and she was weeping on his shoulder and he was muttering a string of appalled comments.

"I didn't mean it... Honest, Amy!... I was just testing...never thought it was true..."

"'Snot," she sobbed, her hands clenched against his chest.

"Not true?" His bewilderment echoed in her ears.

She couldn't bear him thinking she was barren, making her even less of a woman than Steve had left her feeling. She scooped in a deep breath and the necessary words shuddered out. "He didn't want a baby with me."

"Didn't?" He picked up sharply on the past tense.

The betrayal was so fresh and painful, it spilled out. "Having one with her."

"He knocked up some other woman?"

Jake's shock on her behalf soothed her wounded pride. "A bwonde," she explained, her quivering mouth not quite getting around the word.

"Well, I hope you've sent him packing." A fierce admonition, giving Amy the crazy sense he would have done it for her, given the opportunity, probably cracking a bullwhip to effect a very prompt exit.

"Yes," she lied. It was too humiliating to confess she'd sat like a disembowelled dummy while Steve had gone about dismantling and removing his half of their life together.

"Good riddance," Jake heartily approved. "You wouldn't want to have a baby with him, Amy. Couldn't trust a man like that to stick around."

"'Sright." She nodded mournfully, too water-logged to make any cynical parallel to Jake's attitude to women.

"Still feeling raw about it," he murmured sympathetically.

"Yes."

"Guess you only found out this weekend."

"Tol' me Sat'day."

"And I had to slap you in the face with Joshua."

The self-recrimination stirred her to meet him halfway. "Not your fault." There, she'd finally got it out. "Sorry," she added for good measure.

"Don't worry about it, Amy. Bad timing, that's all."

He was being so kind and understanding, patting her on the back, making her feel secure with him, cared for and valued. His warmth seeped into her bones. Her hands relaxed, fingers spreading out across the comforting heat of his chest. She nestled closer to him and he stroked her hair.

Like a wilted sponge, she soaked in his tender compassion, needing it, wanting it. She'd felt so terribly alone these past two days, so bereft of anyone to care about her...

A baby cry pierced the pleasant fuzziness swimming

around in her mind. Joshua! Left alone in the other office! Amy lifted her heavy head, reluctant to push out of Jake's embrace but she couldn't really stay there. Kind understanding only went so far. This was a place of business. A line had to be drawn.

Jake might start thinking she liked being this close to him. In fact, weren't his arms tightening around her, subtly shifting their body contact, stirring a consciousness of how very male he was? To Amy's increasing confusion, she found she wasn't immune to the virility she'd always privately scorned. For several electrifying moments she was mesmerised by its effect on her.

Another baby cry escalated into a wail, demanding attention.

"Responsibility calls, I'm afraid," Jake said wryly, confusing Amy further as he gently loosened his hold on her.

Had she imagined the slight sexual pressure?

He retained one supporting hand at her waist as he lifted his other to tilt her face up. His eyes were a warm, caressing gold. "Got your feet back?" he softly teased.

It drew a wobbly smile. "Firm on the floor again."

"Good!" He nodded approval. The warm molten gold hardened to a glitter. "Better go and wash that guy off your face, as well as out of your mind."

In short, she was a mess and he wanted his personal assistant back in good form. Of course that was all he wanted. Jake Carter was too smart to muddy up his business with pleasures he could get so easily elsewhere.

Then his fingertips brushed her cheek. "Okay?"

Her skin tingled, most probably from the flush of embarrassment rising to her cheeks. ''Yes,'' she asserted as strongly as she could.

He gave her a lopsided grin as he dropped his hand and stepped away. ''The godfather is on duty. Got to see to Joshua.''

He was already at the door before she summoned breath enough to say, ''Thanks, Jake.''

''Any time. My shoulders are broad,'' he tossed at her good-humouredly, heading into his office to tend to his nephew.

Amy took several deep breaths to re-stabilise herself, then forced her legs into action. She picked up her handbag and strode off to the washroom, determined on being what she was supposed to be for Jake. She wouldn't forget his forebearance and kindness, either. Nor the moral support he'd given her. He almost counted as a friend, a solidly loyal friend.

On second thought, she shouldn't go overboard with that sentiment. Jake Carter was her boss. It was more efficient to get his personal assistant back in good working order than to train someone else to meet his needs. She was well aware of Jake's strong dash of pragmatism. Whatever it took to get the end he wanted was meticulously mapped and carried through.

All the same, she deeply appreciated his...well, his sensitivity...to her distress just now. He was also right. She *was* well rid of a man who cheated on her. She should stop grieving and start getting on with the rest of her life.

Though that was easier said than done.

At least she still had her job.

The black hole had closed up before she'd fallen right to the bottom of it, thank God!

Proving she was back in control again, her hand remained absolutely steady as she once more cleaned off her face and re-applied some masterly make-up. Then feeling more in command of herself, she hurried to Jake's office, determined to offer any assistance he required. After all, Joshua was not Steve's baby. She could handle looking after him.

As for Jake…well, she'd been handling him for the past two years. Nothing was going to change there. She just had to keep her head and not let him close to her body again. Business as usual.

CHAPTER FOUR

JAKE had left the door to his office ajar and Amy paused there before entering, amused by the crooning voice he was using for the baby.

"We're on a winning streak now, Josh. Oh, yes, we are, my boyo! We've got Amy Taylor right where we want her."

The smile was jolted off her face by those last words. Though hadn't she known not to trust his benevolence? Jake Carter always took advantage of what was handed to him. Always. If it suited him. One way or another he was going to capitilise on her lapse in professionalism.

"Well, not *precisely* where we want her," he went on.

Good! She'd show him she wasn't putty in his hands. One breakdown didn't mean she was a pushover. She knew where the line was drawn when it came to working with Jake Carter.

"Bit of patience needed, Josh. Bit of manoeuvring. That's a good chap. Hold it right there."

Unsure of how much of this speech applied to her, Amy stepped into the office to take in the scene. The capsule was on the floor and the baby laid out on the bunny rug which had been spread across the desk. Little legs and arms waved haphazardly as Jake triumphantly shoved a used disposable nappy into a plastic bag.

"Clean one coming up," he assured his nephew.

Deciding it was safe to interrupt without giving away the fact she'd been eavesdropping, Amy moved forward to offer the assistance she'd resolved to offer. "Would you like me to take over?"

Jake glanced up and shot her a grin. "Nope. I've got this all figured out." He grabbed Joshua's ankles, raised his bottom off the bunny rug and whipped a clean nappy into place. "Just a matter of getting the plastic tabs the right way around," he informed her.

Since Amy had never changed a nappy in her life, she was grateful Jake had acquired some expertise. It was quite fascinating, seeing the deft way he handled fastening the absorbent pad on the squirming little body.

"You could heat up his bottle for me." Jake waved towards the capsule. "Ruth said to stick it in the microwave for thirty seconds."

"Okay."

Glad to be given something positive to do, Amy quickly found the bottle in the Disney bag and raced off to the kitchenette where she usually made morning or afternoon teas for clients. She wasn't sure what temperature to set on the microwave, decided on medium, then watched the bottle revolve for the required time. A squirt of milk on her wrist assured her it wasn't too hot, and she carried it back to Jake with a buoyant sense of achievement.

Joshua was reclothed and clinging like a limpet to his uncle's shoulder as Jake patted his back. That makes two of us this morning, Amy thought ruefully. Guilt over her earlier refusal to have anything to do with the baby prompted her to offer full services now. Besides which, she didn't want Jake holding anything against her. Power came in many guises, and Jake Carter was a master of all of them.

"I can take him into my office and feed him," she said as *un*grudgingly as she could.

"It's my job," Jake insisted, holding his hand out for the bottle.

She passed it over, frustrated by his righteous stance. Paying *her* back, she thought. Rubbing it in.

"You can read me the mail while I take care of Josh," he added, granting her professional purpose. "I'll dictate whatever needs to be answered or followed through and leave that to you."

"Fine!" she agreed and darted into her office for her notebook, determined not to be faulted again. He already had too much ammunition against her... when he decided to use it.

The man was devilishly clever. She had never trusted him with personal information, suspecting he would somehow wield it to gain more power over her. All along, she had instinctively resisted his strong magnetism, perceiving it as a dangerous whirlpool that sucked people in. Especially women. Amy was in no doubt it paid to be wary around Jake Carter.

She deliberately adopted a business-like air as she seated herself in front of his desk, preparing to sort through the mail with him. However, despite her sensible resolution to take guard, she found the next half hour highly distracting to her concentration on the job.

Jake had settled back in his chair, feet up, totally relaxed as he cradled the baby in the crook of his arm and tilted the bottle as needed for the tiny sucking mouth. He looked so natural about it, as though well practised in the task. He even burped the baby halfway through its feed, propping it on his knee and firmly rubbing its back. Amy herself wouldn't have had a clue how to do that, let alone knowing it should be done.

"Good boy!" Jake crooned as two loud burps emerged, then nestled the baby back in his arm to continue the feeding.

Amy was amazed. Maybe, however improbable it seemed, Jake Carter *was* a staunch family man when it came to his immediate family. Or maybe his self-assurance simply extended to anything he took on. It was all very confusing. She could have sworn she had her buccaneer boss taped to the last millimetre, but he was certainly adding several other shades to his character this morning. Unexpectedly nice shades.

When they'd dealt with the last letter, Amy felt reluctant to leave the oddly intimate little family scene. It was Jake who prompted her, raising a quizzical eyebrow at her silence.

"All finished?"

"Yes."

"Anything I haven't covered?"

"No." She stood up, clutching the letters with her attached notes.

Jake smiled at her, a genuinely open smile, nothing tagged onto it. "Let me know if you run into any problems."

"Okay." She smiled back. Unreservedly.

It wasn't until she was back in her own office with the door closed between them, that it occurred to Amy how much better she was feeling. The day was no longer so gloomy. Steve's betrayal had gathered some distance, making it less overwhelming. She could function with some degree of confidence.

Had she nursed unfair prejudices against her boss?

Had loyalty to Steve pushed her into casting Jake Carter as some kind of devil's advocate who could shake the foundations of a life she valued?

Only one certainty slid out of this musing.

She didn't owe Steve loyalty anymore.

Nevertheless, she'd be courting real trouble if she ever forgot the reasons she'd named her boss Jake the rake!

Amy spent the next half hour diligently working through his instructions, her concentration so intensely focused, she didn't hear the elevator open onto their floor. The knock on her office door startled her. She looked up to see a woman already entering, a tall, curvaceous redhead, exuding an air of confidence in her welcome.

Amy felt an instant stab of antagonism. Some of Jake's women had a hide like a rhinoceros, swanning in as though they owned the place. This one was new. Same kind of sexy glamour puss he usually picked, though—long legs, big breasts, a face that belonged on the cover of *Vogue,* hair obviously styled by a master cutter, very short and chic, designer jeans that clung seductively, a clingy top that showed cleavage.

"Hi! I'm Ruth Powell, Jake's sister."

Amy was dumbfounded. There was no likeness at all. If she hadn't been presented with Jake's nephew this morning, she would have suspected a deception. Some women would use any ploy to get to the man they wanted. Though on closer scrutiny, and with the help of the identification, Amy did see one similarity in the triangular shape of the eyes. The colour, however, was deeper, Ruth's more a sherry brown than yellow-gold.

She had paused beside the door, returning Amy's scrutiny with avid interest. "You're Amy Taylor?" she asked before Amy thought to give her own name.

"Yes," she affirmed, wondering about the testing note in the other woman's voice.

A grin of pure amusement flashed across Ruth's face. "I see," she said with satisfaction.

Perplexed, Amy asked, "See what?"

"Why you dominate so much of Jake's conversation."

"I do?" Amy was astonished.

"So much so that amongst the family we've christened you Wonderwoman," Ruth answered dryly.

Amy flushed, suddenly self-conscious of how less flatteringly she had privately christened Jake.

"Actually, we weren't sure if you were a fire-breathing dragon who kept his machismo scorched, or a stern headmistress who made him toe your line. Now I'll be able to tell everyone you're Irish."

"I'm not Irish," Amy tripped out, feeling more flummoxed by the second.

"Definitely Black Irish." Ruth started forward, gesturing her points as she made them. "You've got the hair, the eyes, and the spirit. You had me pinned like a butterfly for a minute there. Lots of power in those blue eyes."

"I'm sorry if you thought me rude," Amy rushed out, trying to get a handle on this strange encounter.

"Not at all. Call it a revelation. You must have Jake on toast." She laughed, bubbling over with some wicked kind of sibling pleasure as she strolled over to Amy's desk. "I love it. Serve him right."

Amy mentally shook her head. It was an absurd comment—her having Jake on toast. He had enough women to sink a ship. He was hardly dying of frustration because she refused to rise to his bait.

We've got Amy Taylor right where we want her...

The insidious words suddenly took on extra meaning.

With Steve written out of the picture...

Held in Jake Carter's seductive embrace...

But not *precisely* in his bed!

Amy almost rolled her eyes at the totally over-the-top train of thought. Imagination gone wild. Jake's sister obviously enjoyed teasing as much as he did. None of it was to be taken seriously and it was best to put a stop to it.

"I beg your pardon, but..."

"Oh, don't mind me." Ruth twirled one perfectly manicured hand dismissively. "Relief loosening my tongue. I thought Martin's injury was worse that it is. It was hell waiting around in Casualty, fretting over what was happening or not happening."

Martin... that had to be her husband. "His shoulder is all right then?" Amy asked, belatedly recalling it had been dislocated.

"They put it back in. He's sleeping off the anaesthetic now so I thought I'd pick up Josh." Her gaze swept the area behind Amy, frowning at not spotting the capsule. "Where is he?"

"With Jake." Amy nodded towards the connecting door.

Ruth looked her surprise. "You mean he didn't ask you to look after him?"

Amy grimaced. "Well, we had a little contretemps about that. As I understood it, you entrusted him with your baby, so…"

"You insisted he do it?" Ruth's eyes shone with admiration.

"I hope that was right," Amy appealed. "He does seem very good at it."

Ruth broke into laughter again, her eyes twinkling merry approval. "You are priceless, Amy. I'm so glad I got to meet you. As for Jake being good with Josh, he is. Dogs and children gravitate naturally to my brother. So do women. As I'm sure you've noticed," she added with arch understanding.

"Hard not to," Amy returned dryly.

"Too used to getting his own way, my brother."

She was right about that but Amy decided some loyal support was called for. "He does work at it. Not much is left to chance, you know. His background research on every project is very thorough."

"Oh, I wasn't besmirching his professionalism. Jake was always an obsessive perfectionist. A born achiever." Her mouth twitched sardonically. "But some things do tend to fall in his lap."

Like a pile of willing women, Amy silently agreed, but it wasn't her place to say so. She smiled. "Well, Joshua was in his lap, last time I saw him."

"Right! It's been fun talking to you, Amy. Hope to see you again someday," Ruth said warmly, taking her exit into Jake's office.

Fun… Jake's family seemed addicted to fun. Amy

wondered what it might have been like, growing up in that kind of atmosphere. She remembered her own childhood as being dominated by fear of her father. Not that he had ever stooped to physical abuse. He didn't have to. He could cut anyone down with a word or a look. In hindsight, she could identify him as a control freak, but at the time, he was the authority to be escaped from whenever it was possible.

Her mother had been completely cowed. The only escape for her had been in death, and it was her death that had released Amy from staying any longer in her father's household. Her two older brothers had already gone by then, driven away by their father's unreasonable demands. She hadn't seen them in years. She no longer had any sense of family.

What she did have was a strong belief in living life on her own terms. Which was probably why she hadn't pushed for marriage with Steve. The thought of a husband was too closely connected to her father. She didn't want to be owned like that. Ever. In fact, she'd found Steve's much quoted term of being ''free spirits'' very attractive. Until she found out what ''free'' meant to Steve.

What a stupid, blind fool she'd been!

Amy shook her head at herself and turned back to work. There was nothing to be gained by maundering over her mistakes. Her best course was to learn from them and move on. She was briefly tempted to pull out the magazine she'd bought this morning and read the article on exit signs. The thought of Jake catching her at it put her off. No more gaffes today, she sternly told herself.

We've got Amy Taylor right where we want her...

Amy didn't like that smug little boast. She didn't like it at all. She liked *not precisely* much better. She hadn't spent two years honing her defensive skills with Jake Carter for nothing. Whatever he had in mind, she was not going to be a patsy, falling into his lap.

It was Jake who'd made a gaffe, blabbing to the baby. She'd be on her toes from now on, ready to block whatever little one-upmanship game he was planning to play. This time she'd be one step ahead of him.

Yes...she was definitely feeling better.

Jake certainly had a knack of putting zest into her life. Which was a big improvement on the black hole.

CHAPTER FIVE

IT WASN'T long before Jake came in to check how Amy was doing. Ruth had apparently left through his door to the corridor since there was no sight or sound of her and the baby. "On top of it?" he asked casually.

"No problem," she answered, nodding to the print-out of the work she'd done.

He picked up the sheets, then propped himself on the front edge of her desk to read them. As always, his prox-imity put her nerves on edge and she had to concentrate harder on keeping her fingers moving accurately on the keyboard. She was even more aware of him than usual, remembering how he'd held her earlier...his body, his touch. She wondered if he was a sensitive lover.

Her gaze flicked to his hands, the long tapered fingers wrapped around the sheef of paper. They'd stroked her hair so gently. She reminded herself Jake was very smooth at everything he did. Sexual sensitivity didn't necessarily mean he actually cared for the person. Stoking his own pleasure more likely. Though he had seemed to care about her this morning. Had it been en-tirely a pose for an ulterior purpose?

"Couldn't have worded this better myself," Jake said appreciatively. His smile had a caressing quality that al-most made Amy squirm. "You have a great knack of filling out my instructions, Amy, applying the right touch to get through to people without pushing too hard.''

She quelled the whoosh of pleasure at his praise. ''I have been learning off a master the past two years,'' she pointed out, her eyes lightly mocking.

''And an apt pupil you've proved,'' he was quick to add, his admiration undimmed. ''Don't know what I'd do without you. You're my right hand.''

He was laying it on with a trowel. Amy instinctively backed off. ''So what's next on the agenda?'' He was probably buttering her up to land some task he didn't want to do himself in her lap.

''Two years, mmh?'' he mused, ignoring her question. ''You deserve a raise in salary. Ruth is right.''

''About what?'' This was very doubtful ground.

He grinned. ''You're priceless.''

Amy frowned. ''Do you make a habit of discussing me with your family?''

He shrugged. ''Perfectly natural. You are my closest associate. Don't you mention me to yours?''

''I don't have a family.'' It slipped out before she could catch it back.

His eyebrows shot up. ''An orphan?''

The interest beaming at her was not about to be sidetracked. Amy sighed. All this time she'd worked with Jake Carter and managed to keep him at arm's length where any personal issues were concerned. Today she'd blown it in more ways than one.

''Not exactly,'' she muttered, telling herself her family was so far removed from her it didn't matter. ''My mother died when I was sixteen. My father's remarried and we don't get on. I have one brother living in the

U.K., and another settled in Alaska. Hardly what you'd call close.''

Having rattled out the bare facts, Amy constructed a dismissive smile which she found difficult to hold when faced with Jake's appalled reaction.

"You mean you're alone? Absolutely alone with no one to turn to? No backup support?''

"I'm used to it,'' she insisted. "I've been on my own a long time.''

"No, you haven't,'' he fired back at her. "Which was why you were weeping on my shoulder this morning.''

Amy gritted her teeth and glowered at him. "Must you remind me of that?''

"At least *I* was here for you. Just remember that, Amy. When your scumbag of a lover let you down, I was here for you.''

"You're my boss! You weren't here for *me*,'' she argued hotly. "It was purely a matter of propinquity.''

"Nonsense! I took your side immediately. I know what you're worth. Which is a damned sight more than that fool did.''

She knew it! He just had to take advantage of any slip she made. He *revelled in it.* "I do not wish to discuss Steve any further,'' she grated out.

"Of course not. The sooner he's wiped out of your life, the better. Eminently sensible. Though there are practical matters to take into consideration.''

"Yes. Like getting on with work,'' Amy tersely reminded him.

"You might need help in shifting to a new apartment.''

"I like the apartment I've got, thank you.''

"Not a good idea, keeping it, Amy. Memories can be depressing. I realise shifting would be another upheaval you might not want to face right now, but a clean break is the best medicine. Gets rid of the hangover."

"Well, I'm sure you'd know that, Jake," she said with blistering sarcasm.

The acid didn't make a dint. "I'll help you," he said, as though she'd conceded to his argument instead of commenting on his quick turnover in women.

"I don't need your help."

He smiled and blithely waved her protest aside. "Consider me family. It's times like these that family bucks in and picks up the slack. Since I'm the closest thing you've got to family..."

"I do not...remotely...associate you...with family," Amy stated emphatically.

"Well, yes..." One shoulder lifted and fell. Devilment danced into his eyes. "...That probably would be a bit incestuous, wouldn't it?"

"What?" she squawked.

"I can't lie to you, Amy," he declared loftily. "What zips between you and me could not be called sisterly...or brotherly...or motherly...or fatherly."

She flushed, biting her tongue so as not to invite more along this line.

"However, I am genuinely concerned about you," he said, projecting such deep sincerity it swallowed up the devilment and threatened to suck Amy in right after it.

She fought fiercely for a bank of common sense, needing some safe ground between her and Jake Carter. The danger of him infiltrating her private life felt very acute and every instinct told her it wasn't wise. He could bad-mouth Steve as much as he liked but was he any better? His record with women was hardly in his favour!

"I'll ask around," he burbled on. "Find you a nice apartment. Closer to work so you won't have far to travel. Bondi Beach isn't really suitable for you."

"I like Bondi," she protested.

He frowned at her. "Not good for a woman on her own. A lot of undesirables gather out there at weekends. You wouldn't be safe going out at night without an escort."

He had a point, but where was safe at night without an escort? Life without Steve was going to take some adjustment.

"Why not have a look around Balmoral if you want to live by a beach?" Jake suggested. "It's a respectable area. Doesn't draw any trouble."

She rolled her eyes at him and his big ideas. "It's also a very expensive area."

"No more than Bondi. And being on the north side of the harbour, it's much handier to Milsons Point. You won't have to drive across the bridge to work."

"I can't afford it. I can't afford where I am without a partner."

"I said I was upping your salary. Let's say another twenty percent. That should let you live decently."

Amy's mouth dropped open. Her mind flew wildly into calculation mode. "That's more than Steve earns!"

He grinned. "You're worth it. I'll just go and ring a few estate agents I know. See what they can come up with. In the meantime, send these off." He handed her the replies she'd printed out. "They're all fine."

He hitched himself off her desk and left her gaping

after him like a goldfish caught in a bowl, looking out at a foreign world. Jake Carter had always been a shaker and a mover, but never before on her behalf. Was it out of concern for her or did he have other motives up his sleeve?

Amy ran her fingers through her hair, trying to steady the mad whirl in her mind. What could she believe as irrefutable fact? Both Jake and his sister were into game-playing, scoring points. Nothing they said could be taken too seriously.

On the other hand, Jake always delivered what he promised. He wouldn't backtrack on the money. Her salary would now be more than she'd ever dreamed of earning, putting her on a financial level where she was truly independent. Which meant she had options she didn't have before.

A grin broke across her face.

Such a large salary would certainly make her life considerably brighter and it was wonderful to be valued so highly. This morning she'd felt her future had fallen into a black hole, but it wasn't true. There was life after Steve. And she was going to make the most of it, thanks to Jake.

Though if her devious boss was thinking he could attach personal strings to that big hunk of money he'd just handed her, he could think again!

CHAPTER SIX

AMY had just finished filing copies of the letters she'd sent when Jake erupted into her office.

"Grab your handbag," he commanded. "We're off."

"Where to?"

"I'll explain on the way." He checked his watch as he crossed her office to the door. "We've got precisely twenty-five minutes to make the rendezvous."

Amy grabbed her handbag and scooted after him. Jake had the door open for her. She strode into the corridor and summoned the elevator, glad they were going to be involved in some outside activity. Jake would be busy with other people who would take his focus off her and she could get back to feeling relatively normal in his company again.

She always enjoyed these meetings with clients, watching Jake work his brand of magic on them. "Who's the target?" she asked as they stepped into the elevator together.

"Not who. What," he said enigmatically, pressing the ground floor button.

"A new boat?"

He shot her a look of exasperation as the elevator descended. "We do not deal in boats, Amy. Only in yachts," he reminded her.

"Sorry. Slip of the tongue."

"Watch it," he advised darkly. "I want my P.A. to impress the man we're going to meet."

"What's his name?"

"Ted Durkin of Durkin and Harris. Big property dealers."

The name meant nothing to her but clearly it was well known to Jake. The elevator opened onto the reception area before she had time to question him. Jake steered her out and pointed her to the stairwell that led down to the back of the building where he parked his car in a private yard reserved for himself and clients.

"Kate," he called to his front woman, "we're out of the office. Take messages."

"When will you be back?"

"Don't know. If it's anything urgent I can be reached on my mobile."

He hurried Amy down the stairs and outside, using the remote button on his key to unlock the BMW M3 supercar which he currently fancied. Amy headed for the passenger side of the two-door coupe. Haste precluded courtesy. They both took their seats and Jake handed her a folded piece of notepaper as he switched on the ignition.

"What's this?"

"Where we're going. Better get out the Gregory's Street Directory and navigate for me. Haven't got time for wrong turns. I'm right to Military Road. After that, you direct me."

She extracted the guide book from the glove box and settled back for the ride. The scribbled list on the notepaper did not enlighten her as to their destination. In fact, it looked as though Jake had picked up the wrong sheet. What was written appeared to be information about a woman.

Her mouth curled. It seemed he did research on them, as well. "This says, 'Estelle, 26, 8, no smoking, no pets, no WP...'"

"Wild parties," Jake elaborated. "The address is 26 Estelle Road, Balmoral. Apartment 8. The rest are the conditions for rental."

Amy's sardonic humour dried up. Her heart performed a double loop. She waited until it settled back into seminormal rhythm, counting to ten in the meantime. "I take it this is for me," she said as calmly as she could.

"If you like it and if we can swing it."

"Jake, this is not your business." He'd been encroaching on her private life all morning. She had to put a stop to it before it got completely out of hand.

"I said I'd look into it for you," he replied, unshaken from his purpose.

"You said you'd make some calls, not escort me to view places during business hours. I cannot accept..."

"It's almost the lunch hour," he reasoned. "You're always obliging about working overtime in emergencies. The least I can do is this small favour in return."

"This is not an emergency, Jake," she argued, barely holding on to her temper. "I can look for an apartment—if I want to move from the one at Bondi—in my own time."

He frowned at her. "Why are you nit-picking? There's no harm in looking at a place you might like. It could be the ideal change for you."

Amy stubbornly stuck to her guns. "You could have given me the address and…"

"No good! You need me with you for this one. I'm your reference. I pressured Ted into showing it to you ahead of his listing it and he's on his way there now to meet us. He's a handy business contact, Amy. I wouldn't like to waste his time."

She heaved an exasperated sigh, accepting she'd been outmanoeuvred. He was her boss. It would be wrong for her to mess with his contacts. But a stand had to be taken. She didn't want him pulling strings on her behalf, entangling her in them without her knowledge or permission.

"You should have discussed it with me first. I haven't made up my mind on this." And she hated the feeling of being steam-rollered by Jake.

"There's no obligation to take it. Sounded like a great deal for you, though. Worth seeing if it's as good as Ted says. And I might add, he's proved spot-on in his advice to me in the past."

"What's so great about it?" she demanded tersely.

"Location for a start. Ted reckoned it was a pearl for the rent being asked."

"How much?"

He rolled out a sum that was only marginally lower than the rent for the Bondi apartment. Even with her new salary, it would take a bigger chunk of her income than she felt was reasonable for her.

"Ted told me it could command a much higher rent," Jake burbled on. "But the owner's fussy about getting the right tenant in and has scaled the rent to suit. The apartment was recently purchased and is in the process of being refurbished. The owner doesn't want any damage to it, so…''

''No smoking, no pets, no wild parties.'' Amy looked at the list again. ''What does 'SCW' stand for?''

''Single career woman. Someone who respects property and has a tidy mind.'' Jake flashed her a teasing smile. ''I said you fitted the bill. Never met a woman more intent on keeping things in order.''

Including you, Amy thought darkly. He was such a tempting devil, too attractive for his own good, and he thought he could charm his way into anything. Not my life, she fiercely resolved. It was bad enough being dumped by Steve. If she let Jake get too close to her, she had a terrible suspicion he had the power to steal her soul. Then where would she be?

Every self-protective instinct screamed alarm in his presence and today the scream was louder than ever. Raw and vulnerable from the weekend's revelations, Amy admitted to herself she was frightened of Jake slipping past her guard, frightened of the consequences. She fretted over the knowledge he now shared that Steve couldn't be used as a barrier between them anymore.

Though that wasn't entirely right.

Steve had been much more to her than a barrier against Jake.

Much more, she insisted to herself.

She opened the Gregory's Street Directory and started plotting their course to Estelle Street, trying her utmost to ignore the man beside her. His power was threatening to swamp her; powerful masculinity, powerful car, powerful friends, and they were all being used on her. Or so it felt.

We've got Amy Taylor right where we want her.

Not precisely.

A bit of manoeuvring.

The provocative words clicked through her mind again, conjuring up another scenario. An apartment in Balmoral was Jake's idea. He'd given her a raise in salary so she could afford it. He'd found one for her, supposedly to order. He'd tricked her into his car so he could take her there, pressured her with the importance of a business contact.

Was it some kind of put-up job between him and his friendly property dealer, Ted Durkin?

But why?

What good would it do Jake to have her in Balmoral?

He was screwing her up again.

The only way to be sure of anything was to thwart him by making her own decisions her own way. In the meantime she'd play along like a good little girl. Which meant giving directions from the directory.

Amy had never lived on the north side of Sydney and didn't know the Middle Harbour area at all. Her only previous reference to Balmoral was an interview she'd read about a TV celebrity who lived there and loved it. Which undoubtedly meant it was very classy. And expensive. Any place on the harbour was expensive.

Having found Estelle Street on the map, Amy stared at its location with a sense of disbelief. It was only one block back from The Esplanade which ran around the beach. It faced onto a park that extended to The

Esplanade, giving residents a view of greenery, as well an uninterrupted vista of the water beyond it. This had to be a prime location.

She frowned over the rental Jake had mentioned. It was steep for her to pay alone, but it had to be amazingly cheap for an apartment on this street. Even the most run-down place would surely command double that amount, and Jake had said it was being refurbished.

"This doesn't make sense," she muttered.

"What?" Jake inquired.

"I've found Estelle Street. It's almost on the beach. The property there has got to be million dollar stuff. Even with the strict rules, the owner could ask a really high rent."

Jake must have made some under-the-table arrangement with Ted Durkin. She just didn't trust this sequence of events. Or coincidences.

"I did tell you Ted said it was a bargain. For the right person," Jake reminded her. "There is the catch of the six months' lease," he added in the throwaway tone of an afterthought. "But even if this is only a stopgap place for you..."

"What catch?"

She'd been waiting for a "catch." Jake was being altogether too persuasive about this wonderful chance for her. There had to be a "catch."

"Seems the owner plans to take up residence there. Only waiting on selling the current home. Doesn't want to hurry that." He sent her a wise look. "Always best to hang out for the asking price. It's a losing game, selling in haste."

"So it's only for six months."

"Mmh... more like a house-sitter than a tenant, according to Ted. Someone who'll value the place and look after it. Never a good idea to leave a property empty for an extended period of time."

It was beginning to make more sense. Maybe her suspicions were unwarranted. It wasn't beyond the realm of possibility that Jake might want to do her a good turn. If she hadn't overheard those words...was she reading too much into them?

Whatever the truth of the matter, it didn't make a great deal of sense for her to shift house if she had to shift again in six months' time. Changing apartments was a high-cost exercise what with putting up bond money and the expense of moving her furniture, not to mention the hassle of packing and unpacking. Nevertheless, she was curious to see the apartment now. Especially since Jake was investing so much time and talk on it. She still wanted to know why.

They were well along Military Road so she started giving him directions. Within a few minutes he'd made the turns she gave and they were heading down a hill to Balmoral Beach. Amy was entranced by the view. The water was a dazzling blue this morning. A fleet of small yachts were riding at anchor, adding their interest to the picturesque bay. The curved shoreline had a welcoming stretch of clean sand, edged by manicured lawns, beautiful trees and walkways.

This beach had a quiet, exclusive air about it, unlike the broad sweep of Bondi which invited vast public crowds. Even the populated side of The Esplanade looked tidy and respectable, no litter, no grubbiness, not a tatty appearance anywhere. Amy was highly impressed by its surface charm, wishing she had time to explore properly. She made a mental note to come here another day. After all, with Steve gone, she would have plenty of *free* days to do whatever she pleased.

They turned off into the street beside the park and found the address with no trouble at all. The block of apartments was on the next corner, a fairly old block in red brick and only four storeys high with garages underneath. Amy guessed Apartment 8 would be on the top floor, and found herself hoping it was on the corner with the balcony running around two sides, both east and north.

"There's Ted waiting for us," Jake pointed out, waving to the man standing by the entrance to the block.

As they cruised past in search of a parking place, Amy caught only a glimpse of the agent, a broad, bulky figure, smartly attired in a blue business shirt, striped tie, and dark trousers. Jake slotted the car into the kerb only twenty metres away. Amy checked her watch as they alighted. Twelve-thirty. They were on time. Ted Durkin had arrived early. No fault of theirs, but both she and Jake automatically covered the distance at a fast pace.

Amy was conscious of being scrutinised as they approached. It wasn't a sexual once-over, more a matching up to specifications. The agent looked to be in his late forties, his iron-grey hair thinning on top, making his slight frown very visible. It only cleared when Jake thrust out his hand to him, drawing attention away from her.

"Good of you to give us this opportunity, Ted," he enthused genially.

"Not at all. You've put business my way in the past, Jake. Appreciate it."

"This is my P.A., Amy Taylor."

"Pleased to meet you, Mr. Durkin," Amy chimed in, offering her hand.

He took it and gave her a rueful little smile. "To tell you the truth, Miss Taylor, I wasn't expecting someone quite so young."

Single career woman—had he been envisaging a spinsterish woman in her late thirties or forties, someone entrenched in her career with little else in her life?

One thing was suddenly clear. This had to be a *bona fide* deal or Ted Durkin wouldn't be raising questions.

Without pausing to examine her eagerness to dismiss objections to her possible tenancy, Amy rushed to reassure him.

"I'm twenty-eight, Mr. Durkin, and I've held a job since I was sixteen. That's twelve years of solid employment, working my way up to my current position."

"Very responsible," Jake slipped in emphatically.

Ted Durkin shot him a chiding look. "You didn't mention how very attractive your P.A. is, Jake." Another apologetic look at her. "No offence to you, Miss Taylor, but the owner of the apartment was very specific about..."

"No wild parties," she finished for him. "That's not my style, Mr. Durkin."

"Amy's been with me for two years, Ted," Jake said. "I really can vouch for her character. An ultra-clean living person."

"Uh-huh." He raised his eyebrows at her. "No boy-friend? I don't mean to get personal. It's a matter of satisfying the owner. Did Jake explain…?"

"Yes, he did."

Regardless if she was prepared to take the apartment or not, Amy bridled against the sense of being rejected, especially after the painful blow from Steve. She found herself pouring out a persuasive argument, uncaring that it was personal business. Jake knew it anyway and she felt compelled to convince Ted Durkin she was an appropriate tenant.

"Actually I'm looking for time to myself, Mr. Durkin. I've been in a rather long-term relationship which has just broken up." She grimaced, appealing to his sympathy. "No chance of a reconciliation, so I really am on my own and I don't intend rushing into socialising. Six months here would do me very nicely, right away from where I've been."

"Ah!" It was the sound of satisfaction. "Well, I'll take you up and show you around. It's not quite ready for occupation. Painters are in at the moment."

Won a stay of judgement, Amy thought, ridiculously pleased. She glanced at Jake as they entered the building, wanting to share the achievement with him since he'd helped. He wasn't looking at her but she caught a smug little smile on his face and then wanted to kick herself.

She'd ended up playing *his* game, showing positive enthusiasm for *his* plan to move her out of Bondi and to Balmoral.

I was only saving *his* face in front of Ted Durkin, Amy quickly excused herself. She could still say no to the apartment. There was no commitment until she signed the lease for it. In fact, if she decided to move—in her own good time—it was much more practical to find a place that didn't have a time limit on it.

Jake Carter hadn't won this round yet!

CHAPTER SEVEN

THEY rode a small elevator up to the top floor. It opened onto a broad hallway, lit by the multicoloured panes of glass which ran down the opposite wall, making an attractive feature for the stairwell next to it. Ted Durkin ushered them to an opened door on the left hand side. Amy's heart gave an excited skip.

It *was* the apartment with the east-north balconies.

They walked into a wonderfully light, airy, open-plan living area and for Amy it was love at first sight. To live here—if only for six months—it was irresistible—an incredible bargain!

The floor was covered with marvellous tiles, the pearlescent colour of sea-shells crushed into a wavy pattern that instantly suggested a seabed of gently undulating sand. The wall facing the bay was almost all glass, offering a panoramic view and a wealth of sunshine. Other walls were painted a pale cream. The kitchen was shiny new, all blonde wood and stainless steel, fitted with a dishwasher and a microwave oven, as well as a traditional one.

In the living room, two men in paint-spotted overalls sat on foldaway chairs, eating their lunch. A spread-sheet was laid out on the floor underneath them. Tins of paint stood on it in a tidy group.

"How's it going?" Ted asked them.

"One more coat on the skirting boards and architraves and we're finished," the older one answered.

These were being painted a pearly grey, picking up on some of the grains in the tiles and making a stylish contrast to the cream.

"Still wet?"

"Should be touch-dry by now. It's safe to move around."

"Fine." Ted turned to Amy. "The old carpet's been ripped out of the bedrooms for the carpenter to fit the cupboards properly. The new one won't be laid until later this week," he warned.

"There's more than one bedroom?" Amy asked, stunned by the spaciousness of the apartment.

"Two."

Jake wandered over to chat to the painters as the agent steered Amy towards an archway in the back wall of the living room. Apparently he didn't intend to participate in her decision, which made a mess of her line of logic.

She made a determined effort to shake off her pre-occupation with his influence, realising she must have misread the situation, possibly blowing it completely out of proportion. When all was said and done, he had only followed through on what he had advised her. Having her right where he wanted her could simply mean keeping her happy as his assistant.

Through the archway was a short hall with doors at both ends of it and two more doors facing the wall with the arch. The latter pair were opened first. "Laundry and bathroom," Ted pointed out.

The laundry held a linen and broom cupboard, washer, dryer and tub. All new. Amy was delighted to see the washer and dryer since Steve had taken those in the division of their property, leaving her with the refrigerator and the TV. She'd envisaged visits to a laundrette, an inconvenience she wouldn't have to put up with here.

The bathroom was positively luxurious. It had obviously been renovated, the same tiles in the living area being carried through to it and the same blonde wood in the kitchen being used on the vanity bench. Incredibly, it featured a Jacuzzi bath as well as a shower and everything else one could need.

"These old places were built to be roomy. Couldn't put a bath like that in most modern apartments," Ted remarked, probably noting her stunned expression. "You don't often see such high ceilings, either. All the rooms here have bigger dimensions than usual."

And there'd been an enormous amount of money poured into making the most of them, Amy thought. No expense spared. Little wonder that the owner didn't want it damaged by careless tenants.

The second bedroom was larger than average. The main bedroom was larger still, with glass doors that led out onto the north-facing balcony. "What colour is the new carpet?" Amy asked.

Ted shrugged. "Don't know. The owner picked it. I could tell you on Friday."

Amy shook her head. "It doesn't matter. I've never been in such a lovely apartment. Believe me, Mr. Durkin, it would be an absolute pleasure to keep this in mint condition. Do you think the owner will accept me as a tenant?" she pressed eagerly.

His face relaxed into an indulgent smile. His eyes twinkled at her in approval. "Why not? I can sell anything if I believe in it and I'm inclined to believe you, Miss Taylor.''

"I promise your faith won't be mislaid.''

"Well, I do have Jake's word for that, as well, so we'll call it a done deal.''

"Thanks a million, Mr. Durkin.'' She grabbed his hand and shook it vigorously, feeling as though she'd won a lottery.

His smile turned slightly ironic. "Guess you should thank Jake, Miss Taylor. He did the running.''

"Yes, of course. I will.''

Jake! He would probably be insufferably smug about it, but right at this moment Amy didn't care. He'd done her a great favour. A fabulous favour! She floated back out to the living room on a cloud of happy pleasure. The apartment was hers. Six months of blissful living in this beautiful place! It was better than a vacation! New surroundings, new people, new everything!

Jake turned from chatting to the painters and raised his eyebrows at her.

She couldn't help it. She grinned at him like a cheshire cat.

He grinned back.

Understanding zinged between them.

It was like a touch of magic, a fountain of stars showering her, lifting her into a new life. She barely stopped herself from pirouetting across the tiled floor and hugging Jake Carter.

"A done deal?'' he asked.

"A done deal,'' she affirmed exultantly.

"Then let's go to lunch and celebrate,'' he said.

"Yes," she agreed, too happy to worry about caution. Besides, he was part of this. Without Jake she wouldn't have got this apartment. It was only right to share her pleasure with him.

CHAPTER EIGHT

THE restaurant Jake drove her to was on the beach side of The Esplanade, just along from the old Bathers' Pavilion, which he pointed out in passing, informing her it was a historic landmark at Balmoral. Amy smiled over the name. It conjured up men in long shorts and singlets, and women in bathing costumes with skirts and bloomers.

The past, however, was wiped out of her mind as Jake led her into an ultra-modern dining room that shouted class with a capital C. "Table for Carter," he murmured to the woman who greeted them, while Amy was still taking in the huge floral arrangement in the foyer—a splendid array of Australian flora in an urn. The waratahs alone would have cost a small fortune.

Her heels clacked on polished floorboards as Jake steered her into following the woman. Well-dressed patrons sat in comfortable chairs at tables dressed in starched white linen and gleaming tableware. They by-passed a bar that curved around from the foyer and headed towards a wall of glass which seemed to rise from the water beyond it.

This was an illusion, as Amy realised when she was seated right next to the window. There was a strip of beach below them, but they were so close to the waterline, the sense of being right on top of it stayed. Outside, a long wharf was lapped by waves and pelicans were using it as a resting place. Inside, she was handed a menu and asked what she'd like to drink.

"Two glasses of champagne," Jake answered, and gave Amy a smile that fizzed into her blood.

"And a jug of iced water, please," she quickly added, telling herself she needed to keep a cool head here.

She'd been in classy restaurants many times with Jake and a party of his clients, but never before alone with him. The setting engendered a sense of intimacy, as well as a sense of special occasion. A glance at the prices on the menu left Amy in no doubt she was being treated to top class, and the dishes described promised gourmet standard from the chef. She wasn't sure it felt right to be sharing this much with her boss.

"Did you book a table before we left the office?" she asked.

He looked up from his menu, his golden eyes glowing warm contentment. "Yes, I did. Great forethought, wasn't it?" he said with sublime confidence in her agreement.

"There might not have been anything to celebrate," she pointed out.

"Then it would have been a fine consolation for disappointment. Besides, it's lunchtime. On the principle we have to eat, why not eat well? Superb food here. Have you chosen yet?"

"No. It all looks marvellous."

"Good! I figured you needed your appetite tempted. Can't have you pining away on me."

Relieved of any cause for battle, Amy returned her attention to the menu, satisfied she understood Jake's motives. This lunch was part of his program to push her into forgetting her grief and promote the attitude that life was still worth living. Put her in a new environment, lift her spirits with champagne, stuff her up with delicious comfort food, and Amy Taylor would be as good as gold again.

She smiled to herself as she made her choice, deciding on her favourite seafoods. Making the most of Jake's fix-it ideas was definitely the order of the day. He probably didn't have a clue about broken hearts. He never stayed in a relationship long enough to find out. Nevertheless, Amy had to admit he was positively helping her over a big emotional hump.

After this sinfully decadent lunch, they'd be dropping in at Ted Durkin's office to sign the lease on the apartment. She could take up occupation next Saturday. What had loomed as a long, miserable, empty week ahead of her would now be filled with the business of organising the move and coloured with the anticipation of all it would mean to her. To some extent, Jake was right with his practical solutions. Life didn't stay black when good things happened.

Their champagne arrived and their orders were taken. Jake lifted his glass, his eyes twinkling at her over it. "To the future," he toasted.

Amy happily echoed it. "The future. And thanks for everything, Jake. I really appreciate your kind consideration."

"What would I do without your smile? It makes my day."

She laughed at his teasing, then sat back in her chair, relaxing, allowing herself the luxury of viewing him with warmth. "I like working with you," she admitted. "It's never boring."

"Amy, you're the best assistant I've ever had. In fact, you're the perfect complement to me."

He was talking about work, nothing but work, she insisted to herself, yet there was something in his voice that furred the edges of sharp thinking and her heart denied any breakage by hop, skip, and jumping all over the place.

"Jake, darling!"

The jarring intrusion snapped Amy's attention to the woman who had suddenly materialised beside Jake. A blonde! A very voluptuous blonde! Who proceeded to stroke her absurdly long and highly varnished fingernails down Jake's sleeve in a very provocative, possessive manner.

It was like a knife twisting in a fresh wound. Amy could see Steve's blonde getting her claws into him, never mind that he belonged to another woman. A marauding blonde, uncaring of anything but her own desires. This one was insinuating herself between Amy and Jake, splitting up their private celebration party, stealing the lovely comfortable mood, demanding to be the focus of attention.

"What a surprise, seeing you here today!" she cooed to Jake, not asking any pardon for intruding.

Amy hated her. She wanted to tear that hand off Jake's sleeve and shove it into the woman's mouth, shutting off the slavering drool of words.

"An unexpected pleasure, Isabella," Jake returned smoothly, starting to rise from his chair, dislodging her hand.

Isabella! Of course, she'd have a name like that, Amy seethed. Something sexy and exotic.

"No, please stay seated." It was another excuse to touch him, to curl her talons around his shoulder. The blonde bared perfect teeth at Amy. Piranha teeth. "I don't think I've met your companion."

"Amy Taylor...Isabella Maddison," Jake obliged.

"Hi!" the blonde said, the briefest possible acknowledgement.

Amy met her feline green eyes with a chilly blue blast and nodded her acknowledgement, not prepared to play the all jolly friends game. She didn't want to know Isabella Maddison, didn't care to greet an uninvited intruder, and would not pretend to welcome a predatory blonde into her company.

Her and her "Jake, darling!" How rude could you get? It was perfectly obvious the blonde was putting in her claim in front of a possible rival and didn't care what it took to win. Never mind dimming Amy's pleasure, taking the shine off the day, pushing herself forward to block Amy out.

"Great party on Saturday night, Jake," Isabella enthused, giving it a sexy innuendo.

"Yes. A lot of fun," he replied.

Fun! The urge to have a bit of fun herself blew through Amy's mind. "What a pity I couldn't be there!" she said ruefully. "Jake and I have the best fun together, don't we, darling?"

His head jerked to her, eyes startled. He recovered fast, his mouth curving into his whimsical smile. "Ain't that the truth?" he drawled.

'Jake always says we complement each other perfectly," Amy crowed, buoyed so much by his support, she batted her eyelashes at the blonde bombshell.

"Then you should have been there, shouldn't you?" came the snaky return comment, accompanied by a suggestively raised eyebrow.

"Oh, I don't know." Amy shrugged and swirled the champagne around in her glass as she gave Jake a smouldering look. "Some men like a bit of rope. I don't mind as long as I can reel him in whenever I want to."

"Amy is very understanding," Jake said, nodding his appreciation.

"Well, perhaps another time, Jake," Isabella purred, undeterred from a future romp.

"Oh, I doubt it." Amy poured syrup into her voice. "He rarely dips into the same well twice." She bared her teeth. "Take a friendly word of advice. Best to move on to greener pastures. He is sort of stuck with me for the long haul."

Isabella started to retreat. "If you'll excuse me…"

"With pleasure," Amy said to speed her on her way, then downed half the champagne to celebrate her going.

Jake's eyes were dancing with unholy amusement. "My wildest fantasy come true…you fighting another woman for me."

"Huh!" Amy scoffed. "That'll be the day."

"Am I not to believe my ears?"

"She had the wrong coloured hair."

"Ah!" His wicked delight took on a wry twist. "The other woman."

"Sorry if I've queered your pitch with her." She wasn't sorry at all, but it seemed an appropriate thing to say. After all, when all was said and done, he was still her boss. Though he could have stopped her roll if anything important was at stake. She would have taken her cue from him.

"No problem," he said carelessly.

"No, I don't suppose it is." Cynicism streaked through her. "If you snapped your fingers she'd come again."

"Isabella has no claim on me." It was a surprisingly serious statement, and his eyes held hers intently, as though he was assuring her he spoke the truth.

It was meaningless to Amy. No woman ever seemed to have a *claim* on him. "Is she your latest interest?" For some reason, she really wanted to know.

"No," he answered without hesitation.

"Just one of the hopeful crowd that trails after you," Amy said dryly.

He shrugged. "It hardly matters if I'm not interested, does it? To be blunt, Isabella doesn't appeal to me. She never will appeal to me. Any hope she might be nursing is therefore futile."

Goodbye, Isabella.

Amy was pleased that Jake had more taste than Steve. For both the men in her life to fall into the clutches of predatory blondes would have been altogether too wretched to bear. Not that Jake was an *intimate* part of her life, but he was a big chunk and she wanted to respect his judgement of character.

His quirky little smile came back. "You are quite a formidable fighter, Amy."

She shrugged. "You did encourage me, taking my side. If you'd clamped down on me..."

"And miss that performance?" His eyes sparkled admiration.

"The fact remains..." It felt really good that he'd supported her. "...You let me win, Jake."

He lifted his glass of champagne in another toast. "We're a team, Amy. A great team."

"A team," she echoed happily, and drank to the splendid sense of well-being flowing from being a solid team with Jake.

Their first course arrived.

Amy ate with gusto. Not only was the food fantastic, her tastebuds were fully revived from the weekend when everything she'd tried to eat seemed to have the texture of cardboard, indigestible. Maybe having a healthy appetite was a side effect from feeling victorious. Defeat was certainly the pits.

"More champagne?" Jake asked, seeing her down the last drops in her glass.

"No, thanks. I'd better move on to iced water. I think I've been hot-headed enough today."

He grinned. "Some things need letting out of your system. Especially the deep down and poisonous stuff."

"Well, I'm almost squeaky clean again."

"What a shame! So much volatile passion flying around. It's been quite an exciting experience watching it in action. Intriguing, too. Shows me a side of you you've kept under wraps. Not that I didn't suspect it was there."

Amy sat very still because her heart was fluttering extremely fast. Jake was regarding her with simmering speculation. The cat was out of the bag, well and truly, and she'd let it out with her wild flights off the rails. If she wasn't careful, the cat would feel free to pounce!

Twice she'd zoomed out of control, losing any semblance of the cool she'd kept with Jake. She could make excuses for herself. Jake was obligingly accepting them. But that didn't put things back the way they were between them.

"Anything else you'd like to spit out? Get off your chest?" he invited, clearly relishing exploring this newly revealed side of her.

Amy needed a safe topic fast, preferably focused on him instead of her.

"Yes. Since I've now been introduced to your sister, would you mind telling me about your family?" Her curiosity had been piqued by Ruth's revelations this morning.

"Not at all. What do you want to know?"

"Is there only you and Ruth?"

"Ruth is the youngest. I'm the next youngest. Above us are two older brothers, both very respectably settled down with families. Mum does her best to rule over us all and Dad lets us be."

"Do they all live in Sydney?"

"Yes."

"And you're the wild one."

He laughed. "They called me the adventurer when I was a kid."

He still was, Amy thought. "Tell me why," she prompted, eager to know more about him, to understand where he came from.

Again he obliged her, putting her at ease by regaling her with amusing stories from his childhood. Freed from the disturbing sexual pull he could exert on her, Amy enjoyed listening.

It was easy to imagine a little Jake trotting off on his own to explore the exciting things the world had to offer, worrying his mother, trying the patience of his older brothers who were sent to find him after they'd neglected to mind him properly. Ruth had become his partner in voyages of wonder when she was old enough, happy to be led anywhere by Jake.

The first course was cleared from their table. The main course was served and consumed. They were both per-suaded to order the divine-sounding apple and brandy soufflé served with a lemon and kiwi fruit compote to finish off the meal.

The stories went on, eagerly encouraged by Amy. Hearing about a happy childhood, and a family that wasn't in any way dysfunctional, was something new to her, almost magical. She tended not to think about her own—no happy memories there—and Steve had been an only child whose parents had divorced when he was eight. He'd virtually lived in a world of computer games through his teens and they were still an escape for him whenever an argument loomed.

She wondered if his blonde knew that about the man she'd snaffled. Avoidance was Steve's answer to con-frontation. Which was probably why Amy had been pre-sented with his fatherhood and the date of his marriage, showing in one inarguable stroke there was no point in fighting.

Anything for a peaceful life. Steve's philosophy. She'd thought it was good but it wasn't really. Problems never got properly aired.

"I've lost you."

Jake's dry comment drew her attention back to him. She smiled. "No. I was just thinking how lucky you are not to have any fears. Or inhibitions. You were very blessed being born into your family, Jake."

He cocked his head slightly. The speculation in his eyes gradually took on the wolfish gleam that usually played havoc with her nerves. Maybe she'd been lulled by her good fortune, the champagne and fine food. Instead of alarm, she felt a tingling thrill of challenge.

"Everyone has fears, Amy," he drawled. "And inhibitions are placed upon them, whether they want them or not."

"Like what?" she said recklessly.

"Well, take you and me. I'd like nothing better than to race you off to bed and make mad passionate love for the rest of the afternoon."

For one quaking moment, Amy was tempted.

Then Jake gave his quirky smile and added, "But if I had my wicked way, I'm afraid you might bolt out of my life, and I wouldn't like losing you. So here I am…hopelessly inhibited."

The soufflés arrived.

"Consolation," Amy said, doing her utmost to hide both the shock and the relief she felt.

Jake laughed and picked up his spoon. *"Bon appétit!"*

Off the hook, Amy thought gratefully. The temptation had come so swiftly and sharply, she was still quivering inside. She sternly bent her mind to reasoning it away.

It was because the physical attraction had always been there, and with Steve's defection, pursuing it was no longer forbidden. And it felt great having Jake at her side, fighting on her behalf against Steve, against the blonde, treating her as though she was precious to him.

But it would be crazy—absolutely crazy—to get sexually involved with Jake. She'd only be one of an endless queue—another little adventure—and how on earth would she be able to work with him afterwards? She'd hate it when he dumped her and took up with someone else. As he surely would.

Besides, she didn't really want to make love with him. It was just that he'd made her feel desirable, like a winner instead of a loser and a reject. It was simply a seductive situation. And he'd thought better of it, too, applying solid common sense.

Here she was on a winning streak and it would be really silly to spoil it. Today had brought her a wonderfully ego-boosting salary, and an apartment that was close to paradise. However tempting it might be to add a new lover to the list, it was best to get any thought of tangling with her boss in bed right out of her mind.

She put down her spoon and then realised she'd shovelled the soufflé down her throat without really tasting it. Wasted, she thought. Which was a pity. A delight missed.

A glance across the table showed Jake had finished his, too. She didn't know for how long but she suddenly felt him keenly observing her and had the awful sense he'd been reading her thoughts. She glanced at her watch, anxious to divert any further disturbing exchanges between them.

"Good heavens! The afternoon's almost gone!" Her gaze flew to his in sharp appeal. "We'd better leave, Jake."

He checked his watch, raising his eyebrows in surprise. "You're right. Got to get that lease signed on our way back to the office." He signalled for the bill and smiled at Amy. "A good day's work."

She laughed, trying to loosen up. "We've played hookey for hours."

"There's a time and place for everything," he answered blithely.

And this wasn't quite the time and place...yet...for what he had in mind.

Amy tried to scotch the thought but it clung. "I'll just make a quick visit to the powder room," she said, rising from the table, hoping she wasn't appearing too skittish.

"Fine. I'll meet you in the foyer."

She had her armour in place when she emerged from the powder room. Jake was waiting, looking well satisfied with his world. He wasn't about to race her off, not without appropriate encouragement from her, anyway. She was safe with him as long as she kept herself under control.

"What's the name of this restaurant?" she whispered as they headed outside.

"The Watermark."

"Ah! Very appropriate. It was a wonderful lunch, Jake. Thank you."

"I enjoyed it, too."

No doubt about that, Amy thought. The teasing twinkle in his eyes was not the least bit dimmed. Jake Carter always lived to fight another day. He settled her in his car with an air of the man in possession.

But he wasn't.

Thanks to Steve, Amy *was* a free spirit.

The name of the restaurant lingered in her mind as they drove towards completing the business of the day. *The Watermark*... It made her think of tides. When one rolled out, another rolled in. High points, low points. She wondered if making love with Jake Carter would be like eating a soufflé—a delight and then nothing.

Sex without love.

Forget it, she told herself.

Missing it didn't hurt her one bit.

CHAPTER NINE

AMY did her best to carry a positive attitude home with her that evening. She didn't allow the emptiness of the apartment she'd shared with Steve swamp her with depression. Soon it would be empty of both of them, she told herself. This phase of her life was over. Another was starting and she was going to make the most of it.

She made lists of what had to be done; contact the agency that handled the Bondi apartment and give notice of moving, telephone and electricity bills to be finalised, look up removalists and get estimates, collect boxes for packing. She was mentally arranging her furniture in the new Balmoral apartment when the telephone rang, jolting her back to the present.

Amy felt reluctant to answer the call. It might be for Steve, someone who didn't know he was gone, and she would have to explain. Shock and sympathy would follow and she'd be forcefully reminded of her grief and humiliation. She glared at the telephone, hating its insistent burring, wanting to be left alone to pick up her new life.

The summons finally stopped. Amy sighed in relief. Maybe it was cowardly not to face up to the truth, but it was such a hurtful truth she just wanted to push it aside. To her increasing chagrin, however, she was not left in peace. The telephone rang on and off for the next hour, demanding an answer. She balefully considered taking the receiver off the hook, then realised that could instigate an inquiry from the telephone company since the caller was being so persistent.

In the end, the need to cut off the torment drove her to snatch up the receiver. "Amy Taylor," she snapped into it.

"Thank heaven! I was getting really worried about you, Amy. It's Brooke Mitchell here."

Brooke! Amy instantly grimaced. Her least favourite person amongst her acquaintances.

"When Ryan came home from work and told me what Steve had done, I just couldn't believe it at first," she blathered on. "Then I thought of you and how you must be feeling, you poor dear..."

"I'm fine," Amy interrupted, recoiling from the spurious gush of sympathy.

Gush of curiosity more like! Brooke Mitchell lived for gossip, revelled in it, and Amy had never really enjoyed her company. Brooke just happened to be married to Ryan who worked with Steve and the two men were both computer heads, moving their common interest into socialising occasionally.

"Are you sure? When you weren't answering the phone..."

"I've only just come in," Amy lied.

"Oh! I had visions of you...well, I'm relieved you haven't...uh..."

"Slit my wrists? I assure you I'm not the least bit suicidal, Brooke. No drama at all." *For you to feed off,* Amy silently added.

"I didn't mean...it's just such devastating news. And I can't say how sorry I am. I don't know how Steve could have done it to you. Infidelity is bad enough but getting the woman pregnant and deciding to marry her...after all the years you've been together..."

Amy gritted her teeth. Brooke was rubbing salt into the wound.

"...It's just terrible," she went on. "Though I've never thought living together was a good idea. You should have nailed him down, Amy. It's the only way to be sure of them."

It was the smug voice of a married woman. Amy refrained from saying divorce statistics didn't exactly prove Brooke right. It would have sounded like sour grapes.

"If you need a shoulder to cry on..."

The memory of Jake holding her brought a sudden rush of warmth, taking the nasty chill off this conversation. "I'm really fine, Brooke. In fact, I've had a lovely day. Jake Carter, my boss, took me out to lunch to celebrate my new freedom."

Which was almost true.

"You told him about Steve?" Real shock in her tone this time.

Caught up on a wave of bravado, Amy ploughed on in the same vein. "Yes, I did. And Jake convinced me I was well rid of him, so don't be concerned about me, Brooke."

"I see." Doubt mixed with vexation at this turn of events. "Didn't you tell me your boss was a rake?"

"Mmh. Though I'm thinking it might well be a worthwhile experience being raked over by Jake Carter."

"Amy! Really!"

"Yes. Really," she echoed, determined on wiping out

any image of her being thrown on the scrap heap, too crushed to raise any interest in another man.

"Well..." Brooke was clearly nonplussed. "I was feeling so awkward about bringing up next Saturday's party. I mean, when I invited you and Steve, I expected you to be together. Now...well, it is awkward, Amy. Ryan says Steve will want to bring..."

"Yes, of course," Amy rushed in, her heart contracting at the thought of the pregnant blonde on Steve's arm, queening it in Amy's place. And the plain truth was, Steve was far more Ryan's friend than she was Brooke's.

"But if you want to bring Jake Carter..." Her voice brimmed over with salacious interest.

"I was about to say I have other plans, Brooke. It was kind of you to be concerned about me and I'm glad you called. I'd forgotten about the party. Please accept my apologies. And I do wish you and Ryan a very merry Christmas."

She put the receiver down before Brooke could ask about her plans, which were none of the other woman's business. It gave Amy some satisfaction to think of Brooke speculating wildly about Jake, instead of pitying her, but it had probably been a rash impulse to use him to save her pride. The word would be quickly spread...

So what? Amy thought miserably. It would probably salve everybody's unease about excluding her from future activities. Brooke had been angling to cancel the party invitation and she wouldn't be the only one to dump Steve's ex-partner in favour of his wife-to-be.

When couples broke up, it forced others to make choices and the pragmatic choice was to accept a couple rather than a suddenly single woman who could either be a wet blanket at a social gathering or a threat to other women's peace of mind.

Depression came rolling in as she realised she was now a social pariah and she didn't really have friends of her own. The five years of sharing her life with Steve had whittled them away, and the past two years as Jake's personal assistant had kept her so busy, she literally hadn't had the time to develop and nurture real friendships. In fact, she felt closer to her boss than she did to anyone else at the present moment, and that brought home what a sorry state she was in.

Jake had filled the emptiness today but she knew how foolish it would be to let herself become dependent on him to fill her future. She had to take control of her own life, find new avenues of meeting people. The need-to-do list she'd made seemed to mock her. It would get her through the next week, but what then?

Amy couldn't find the energy to think further. She went to bed and courted oblivion. Being without Steve had to get easier, she reasoned. Everyone said time was a great healer. Soon she'd be able to go to bed and not think of him cuddled up to his blonde. In sheer defence against that emotional torment, she started visualising what it might be like to be cuddled up with Jake Carter. It was a dangerous fantasy but she didn't care. It helped.

Though it didn't help her concentration on work the next day. It made her acutely aware of every physical aspect of the man, especially his mouth and his hands. Even the cologne he wore—a subtle, sexy scent—was an insidious distraction, despite its being the same cologne he always wore. It didn't matter how sternly she berated herself for imagining him in Steve's place, the fantasy kept popping into her head, gathering more and more attractive detail.

It was terribly disconcerting. Thankfully, Jake didn't notice how super-conscious she was of him. He seemed totally tied up with business, not even tossing her teasing remarks. Certainly there was no allusion to any wish to race her off and make mad passionate love, nor any suggestion it was on his mind.

Amy hoped her stupid boast to Brooke Mitchell would never reach his ears. Not that she'd meant it. It was purely a reaction to circumstances, not a real desire. She knew better than to actually *want* Jake Carter in her bed. In the flesh.

The only personal conversation came at the end of the day as she was preparing to leave. Jake stood in the doorway between their offices, watching her clear her desk. "Are you holding up okay, Amy?" he asked quietly.

She flushed at the question. "I am *not* suicidal!" she snapped, the conversation with Brooke all too fresh in her mind, plus everything else that had flowed from it.

Jake's eyebrows shot up. "The thought never entered my mind."

"Then why ask?" she demanded, dying at the thought he'd noticed how jumpy she was around him.

His mouth quirked. "Guess you've already had well-meaning friends nattering in your ear."

"You could say that."

"Do you still plan to move house on Saturday?"

"Absolutely. Saturday can't come fast enough."

The quirk grew into a grin that seemed to say *That's*

my girl! and Amy's heart pumped a wild stream of pleasure through her body, spreading a warm, tingly feeling.

"You seemed rather unsettled today," he remarked with a shrug. "It made me wonder if there was too much on your plate. Moving can be a hassle if you intend to do it without the help of well-meaning friends."

"I've got it all lined up," she informed him, although it wasn't quite true. She had spent the lunch hour on the telephone, organising what she could.

"Fine! If you need some time off, just ask. If there's anything I can do to facilitate the resettling process..."

"Thanks, Jake." She smiled, relieved he'd put her edginess down to her emotional state over Steve. "I think I can manage but I'll let you know if I need some time off."

He nodded, apparently satisfied. "One other thing, Amy. You know we've sent out brochures and invitations to the New Year's Eve cruise on *Free Spirit.*"

"Yes." The magnificent yacht came instantly to mind, pure luxury on water. The cruise, which would feature the fireworks display over the harbour on New Year's Eve, had a guest list of potential clients, all of whom could be interested in chartering the yacht for either business or pleasure. As Jake had it planned, New Year's Eve was the perfect showcase for *Free Spirit.*

"Well, if you're not tied up that evening, I'd really appreciate your hostessing for me on the yacht. I know it's work on a holiday night, but you would get a front-line view of the fireworks and they're supposed to be the best ever."

Amy barely heard his last words. Her mind was stuck

on *not tied up*. Steve would certainly be tied up. It was his wedding night. He and his blonde bride would be...

"I'll be happy to hostess for you," she rushed out, welcoming any distraction from those thoughts and the curdling that had started in her stomach.

"Thanks, Amy. It should be a most productive evening."

No, it won't, she thought. The production was already in place. The only difference would be the wedding rings, holding it together.

"And a fun time, as well," Jake went on.

Fun! Well, she could always fall overboard and drown herself. Except she wasn't suicidal.

"You can count on me," she said dully.

"Good!" He gave her a casual salute. "Happy packing."

It was more a case of ruthless packing, than happy. In sorting through the contents of drawers, Amy discovered Steve had left behind all the photographs of their life together, as well as mementos from their skiing trips and seaside vacations. She threw them out. Threw out the clothes that reminded her of special occasions, too. If he could walk away from it all, so could she.

When tears occasionally fell over silly, sentimental things, she dashed them away, determined on not faltering in her resolution. It occurred to her that death would be easier to accept than betrayal. At least you were allowed to keep good memories when someone died, but all her memories of Steve were tainted now. She could never again feel *good* about him. Best to let him go. Let the hurt go, too.

Unfortunately, however hard she worked at achieving

that end, she couldn't make the awful sense of aloneness go. Even the strong connection she felt with Jake Carter was not enough to dispel it. That couldn't be allowed to progress to real intimacy, so the pleasure of it was always mixed with a sense of frustration. Which added to her feeling of defeat, as though she was fated to be drawn to men who would never ultimately satisfy her.

She welcomed the weekend, eager for the move to Balmoral and the change it would bring to her life. No one except Jake knew about it. Easier to cut her losses, she'd argued to herself. Those who might try to contact her were all connected to Steve and she guessed that any caring interest would quickly fade once she was completely out of the picture. In any event, it was better for her to move on.

She did not regret walking out of the Bondi apartment for the last time on Saturday morning. It was a glorious summer day, an appropriate omen to leave gloom behind and fly off to the *wide blue yonder*. She smiled over her use of Jake's company name. It did have a great ring to it, promising an adventure that obliterated the greyness of ordinary day-to-day life.

As she followed the removalist's van across the Sydney Harbour Bridge, her spirits were buoyed by the sense of going somewhere new and exciting, and when she arrived at Balmoral, it was every bit as lovely as she remembered it. So was the apartment.

She did, however, have an odd sense of *déjà vu* on looking into the master bedroom. The new carpet was turquoise, almost the exact shade as used in the offices at Milsons Point. Then she realised the paintwork was similar, too. It felt uncanny for a moment, almost as if

Jake had left the imprint of his personality here. But the colours were easy to live with and an attractive combination. Anyone could have chosen them.

Having already planned where to place her furniture, Amy was able to direct the removalist men efficiently. They came and went in very short time. She spent the rest of the day, unpacking suitcases and boxes, exulting over how much space she had in cupboards and arranging everything to please herself.

When she was finally done, fatigue set in, draining her of the excitement that had kept her fired with energy. She was here, old shackles cut, bridge crossed, ready to write a new page in her life, yet suddenly it didn't mean as much as she wanted it to. There was no one to show it to, no one to share it with, and the black beast of loneliness grabbed her again.

She wandered around, still too wired up to relax. Watching television didn't appeal. She plumped up the cushions on her cane lounge suite, eyed its grouping with the small matching dining setting, and knew she'd only be fiddling if she changed it. The view should have soothed her but it didn't. Somehow it imbued her with the sense of being in an ivory tower, separated from the rest of the human race.

The ringing of her doorbell made Amy almost jump out of her skin. A neighbour? she wondered. Even a stranger was a welcome face right now. In her eagerness to make an acquaintance, she forgot to take precautions, opening the door wide and planting a smile on her face.

Jake Carter smiled back at her.

Jake, exuding his charismatic sexiness, looking fresh and yummy and sun-kissed in an orange T-shirt and white shorts, lots of tanned flesh and muscle gleaming at her, taunting her with its offering of powerful masculinity, accessible masculinity, his wicked, yellow wolf's eyes eating up her dishevelled state and his smile saying he liked it and wouldn't mind more.

Amy's impulses shot from wanting to hug him for coming, to a far wilder cocktail of desires running rampant. Or was it need clawing through her? It was madness, anyway. She felt virtually naked in front of him, clothed only in skimpy blue shorts and a midriff top that she usually wore to her aerobics class. Quivers were attacking her stomach and her breasts were tightening up. Indeed, she felt her whole body responding to the magnetic attraction of his.

It was scary.

Alarming.

And the awful part was she sensed he knew it and wasn't the least bit alarmed by it. He was positively revelling in it. And he'd come here at this hour, when she was so rawly vulnerable, having burnt all her bridges, making himself available to her, seeking entry…Jake, the rake.

The moment those words slid into her mind, sanity bolted back into it, repressing the urges that had been scrambling common sense. In sheer, stark defence, words popped out of her mouth, words she would have given anything to take back once they were said, but they hung there between them, echoing and echoing in her ears.

"I'm not going to bed with you."

CHAPTER TEN

"ACTUALLY, I was thinking about feeding other appetites," Jake drawled, holding up a plastic carrier bag that held takeaway containers and a paper bag bulging with bottles of wine.

Amy flushed scarlet. She knew it had to be scarlet because her whole body felt as though it was going up in flames. Even her midriff.

"First things first," Jake burbled on. "Moving is a hot, thirsty business and you've probably been run ragged today, too tired by now to think of bothering with a proper dinner, even if you did get provisions in."

Which she hadn't, except for absolute basics.

"And since you insisted on doing all this on your own, I thought you might welcome company at this point. Winding down at the end of the day, putting your feet up, enjoying some tasty food and a glass of wine…"

He was doing it to her again, pouring out a reasonable line of logic she couldn't argue with. Except he was here at the door of her home. And it wasn't business hours. And he certainly wasn't dressed for business. This was personal.

With Jake Carter, personal with a woman meant…

His eyes twinkled their devilish mischief. "But if you want to change your mind about going to bed with me later on in the evening…"

"There! I knew it!" she shot at him triumphantly, having worked her way out of the hot fluster.

"Whatever you decide is okay by me, Amy," he blithely assured her. "I wouldn't dream of going where I wasn't wanted."

"I didn't invite you here, Jake," she swiftly pointed out.

"Telepathy," he declared. "It's been coming at me in waves all day. Couldn't ignore it."

"I haven't thought of you once!"

"Subconscious at work. No one here to share things with. Low point coming up."

Suspicion glared back at him. "Sounds more like psychology to me." *Get the girl when she's down!*

"Well, you could be right about that," he grandly conceded. "I guess I was compelled by this sense of responsibility towards you."

"What responsibility?"

"Well, I said…Jake, my boy, you more or less pushed Amy into that apartment. There she is, without her familiars, and the least you can do is turn up and make sure she's okay."

"I'm okay," she insisted.

His mouth moved into its familiar quirk. His woman-trap eyes glowed golden with charming appeal. "I brought dinner with me."

No one, Amy reflected, knew the art of temptation better than Jake Carter. She could smell the distinct aroma of hot Chinese mixtures. Her stomach had unknotted enough to recognise it was empty. More to the point, sparring with Jake had banished the black beast of loneliness. If she sent him away…

"Dinner does sound good," she admitted.

"I hate eating alone," Jake chimed in, pressing precisely the button that had Amy wavering.

"I wouldn't mind sharing *dinner* with you," she said with arch emphasis.

"Sharing is always better." He cocked an eyebrow in hopeful appeal. "Can I come in now? I promise I won't even ask you to show me the bedroom."

No, he'd just sweep her off there, Amy thought, and the awful part was, the idea had a strong attraction. But he didn't know that...couldn't know it...and she was making the rules here.

"Be my guest," she said, standing back to wave him in. "You know where the kitchen is," she urged, not wanting him to linger beside her.

He breezed past, never one to push his luck when the writing was on the wall. As Amy shut the door after him, it occurred to her she might be driving the loneliness beast out, but she'd let the wolf in, a wolf who'd huffed and puffed very effectively, blowing her door down, so to speak.

On the other hand, he wasn't about to eat her for dinner. He'd brought Chinese takeaway. She could manage this situation. But she wouldn't feel comfortable staying in these clothes. She was too...bare.

Jake was happily unpacking his carrier bag, setting out his offerings along the kitchen counter. His white shorts snugly outlined the taut curve of particularly well-shaped buttocks. When it came to cute butts, Jake Carter could line up against any gym buff. As for power-packed thighs... Amy took a grip on herself, wrenching her mind off the seductive promise of so much impressive male muscle.

Looks weren't everything.

So what if Steve had been on the lean side in comparison?

"Lemon chicken, sweet and sour pork, Mongolian lamb, braised king prawns, chilli beef, fried rice." Jake shot her a dazzling grin as he finished listing his menu. "All ready for a banquet."

"Good choice," she commented as blandly as she could.

. He laughed. "I have acquired some knowledge of your preferred tastes, Amy."

It surprised her. "You noticed?"

"There isn't much I haven't noticed about you in the two years you've been at my side." His gaze skated over her skimpy clothes. "Though I haven't seen you look quite so fetching as you do this evening. Very *au naturel.*"

Amy instantly folded her arms across her midriff but she was acutely aware the action didn't hide the tightening of her nipples.

His eyes teased the flare of hard defence in hers. "Just as well I'm a man of iron control."

The need for evasive action was acute. "I was about to take a shower and clean up."

"Go right ahead." He waved expansively. "Make yourself comfortable. I'll get things ready for us here."

If he thought she was going to reappear in a sexy negligee, he was in for severe disappointment.

All the same, as Amy stood under the shower, soaping off the stickiness of the long, humid day, she couldn't help wondering how well she stacked up against Jake's other women. Thanks to her aerobics classes and a healthy diet, she was in pretty good shape, no flab or cellulite anywhere. No sag in her breasts.

She'd always been reasonably content with her body and normally she wasn't self-conscious about being nude. Not that she intended stripping off for Jake Carter. Besides which, he probably only fancied her because she remained a challenge to him. What physical attributes she had were really irrelevant.

With Jake it was always the challenge. Had to be. Which was why he lost interest once he'd won. At least, that was how it looked to Amy. Though she couldn't see there was much winning in it when women fell all over him anyway.

She decided to wash her hair, as well. It would do him good to wait. Show him she was not an eager beaver for his scintillating company. Besides, she felt more in control if she was confident of her appearance; fresh, clean, tidy, and properly clothed.

By the time she finished blow-drying her hair it was full of bounce and so was she, looking forward to keeping Jake in his place. She left her face bare of make-up since she wasn't out to impress. Jake could have that part of her *au naturel.*

Deciding jeans and a loose T-shirt would make a clear statement—demure and dampening—she tied the belt firmly on her little silk wraparound for the dash from bathroom to bedroom, opened the door to the hallway, and was instantly jolted from her set plan by a flow of words from Jake.

"She's in the shower, making herself comfortable."

He had to be talking to someone.

"Would you like a glass of champagne?" he burbled on, apparently having invited the someone into her apartment! "I've just poured one for Amy and myself."

"What the hell is going on here?"

The incredulous growl thumped into Amy's heart. It was unmistakably Steve's voice!

"Pardon?"

"Amy can't afford a place like this." Angry, belligerent suspicion.

The shock of hearing her ex-partner gave way to a fierce wave of resentment. How dare he judge or criticise!

"I gave her a raise in salary," Jake blithely replied. "She deserved it. Best P.A. in the world. Is it yes to the champers?"

"No. I only came to see that she was all right."

Guilt trip, Amy thought, writhing over how she'd been so hopelessly devastated last week.

"From the look of it I could have saved myself the trouble," he went on, the sneer in his voice needling Amy beyond bearing.

She whirled through the archway in a rage of pride, coming to a stage-stop as she took in the scene, Jake by the table he'd set for their dinner, brandishing a bottle of champagne, Steve standing by the kitchen counter, keeping his distance, obviously put out by her luxurious living area and Jake's presence.

His carefully cultivated yuppie image—the long floppy bang of hair dipping almost over one eye, the white collarless linen shirt and black designer jeans—somehow looked immature, stacked up against the raw male power so casually exhibited by Jake, and for once Amy was pleased Steve came off second-best in comparison. She fully intended to rub it into her ex-lover's ego. Let *him* be flattened this time!

"Good heavens! How on earth did you get here, Steve?" she trilled in amazement.

He gawped at her, making her extremely conscious of her nakedness under the silk and lace bit of froth, which, of course, he recognised as part of the seductive and sinfully expensive lingerie she'd bought herself for her last birthday, intending to pepper up their sex life. The outcome had been disappointingly limp, undoubtedly because he'd been bedding the blonde.

"Mmmh..." The sexy purr from Jake was meant to inflame. "I love your idea of comfortable."

"I'm so glad," she drawled, seized by the reckless need to prove she wasn't a downtrodden cast-off. Abandoning all caution, she ruffled her squeaky-clean hair provocatively as she sauntered towards Jake, knowing full well the action would cause a sensual slide of silk over her curves. "Champagne poured?"

"Ready to fizz into your bloodstream, darling."

The wicked wolf eyes were working overtime as he handed her a brimming glass. One thing she could say for Jake, he was never slow on the uptake. Right at this moment, his response was positively exhilarating. In the hunk stakes, Jake Carter was a star.

"Darling!" Steve squawked.

Hopefully he was feeling mortifyingly outshone! And very much the odd one out in *this threesome!*

"I've always thought she was," Jake tossed at him. "I should thank you for bowing out, Steve. It freed Amy up for me, got rid of her misplaced loyalty, opened her eyes..."

"I didn't do it for you," Steve chopped in, furious at finding himself upstaged by her boss.

"Which reminds me, where is your bride-to-be?" Amy asked silkily, having fortified herself with a fine slug of alcohol. "Lurking outside to see that you don't stay too long?"

"No, she's not!"

"Well, if I were her, I wouldn't trust you out of my sight. Not after working so hard to get a ball and chain on you."

Let his *free spirit* wriggle on that barb, Amy thought bitterly. She sipped some more champagne to dilute the upsurge of bile from her stomach.

Steve's face bloomed bright red. To Amy, it was a very satisfying colour. Much better than the pallid white he'd left on her face a week ago.

"She knows I'm here. I told her..."

"And just how did you know where to come, Steve?" she inquired with sweet reason. "I haven't given this address to anyone."

"Except me," Jake popped in, shifting to slide his arm around her shoulder in a man-in-possession hug. "We've moved so much closer in the past few days."

Amy snuggled coquettishly, getting quite a charge out of the hip and thigh contact.

Steve looked as if he was about to burst a blood vessel. Which served him right, having thrown a blonde and a baby in her face. He clenched his jaw and bit out his explanation.

"I went to the Bondi apartment this morning and saw our stuff being carried out to the removalist van..."

"*Our* stuff?" She couldn't believe he was backtracking on the division of their property. How crass could he get in the circumstances? "It was agreed this was *my* stuff."

"Mostly, yes. But there were little things I left behind. Overlooked in...well, not wanting to make things worse for you."

"Worse for whom?" she demanded with arch scepticism. "The great evader couldn't get out fast enough. That's the truth of it, Steve."

He flushed. "Have it your way. But I still want my things. And since you'd obviously packed up the lot, I followed the van here, then gave you time to unpack..."

"How considerate of you! What things?"

"Well, there were photographs and mementos..."

"I threw them all out."

"You...what?"

Amy shrugged. "Unwanted baggage. What's gone is gone," she declared and proceeded to drain her glass as though to celebrate the fact.

"One never enjoys being reminded of mistakes, Steve," Jake remarked wisely.

"You could have called me first," Steve spluttered accusingly.

"Sorry." She slid a sultry look up at Jake. "I've been somewhat distracted this week."

He instantly brushed his mouth over the top of her hair, murmuring, "Amy, I've got to tell you that scent you wear is extremely stimulating."

She wasn't wearing any scent. Unless he meant her

PLAY "LUCKY 7" AND GET
THREE FREE GIFTS!

HOW TO PLAY:

1. With a coin, carefully scratch off the silver box at the right. Then check the claim chart t see what we have for you — **FREE BOOKS** and a gift — **ALL YOURS! ALL FREE!**

2. Send back this card and you'll receive brand-new Harlequin Presents® novels. Thes books have a cover price of $3.75 each in the U.S. and $4.25 each in Canada, but they ar yours to keep absolutely free.

3. There's no catch. You're und no obligation to buy anything. W charge nothing — ZERO — f your first shipment. And you dor have to make any minimum numb of purchases — not even one!

4. The fact is thousands of readers enjoy receiving books by mail from the Harlequ Reader Service® months before they're available in stores. They like the convenience home delivery and they love our discount prices!

5. We hope that after receiving your free books you'll want to remain a subscriber. B the choice is yours — to continue or cancel, any time at all! So why not take us up on o invitation, with no risk of any kind. You'll be glad you did!

YOURS FREE!

PLAY LUCKY 7 FOR THIS EXCITING FREE GIFT!

THIS SURPRISE MYSTERY GIFT COULD BE YOURS FREE WHEN YOU PLAY

LUCKY 7!

PLAY THE

7

LUCKY

SLOT MACHINE GAME!

Just scratch off the silver box with a coin. Then check below to see the gifts you get!

YES!

306 HDL CPQ4

I have scratched off the silver box. Please send me all the gifts for which I qualify. I understand I am under no obligation to purchase any books, as explained on the back and on the opposite page.

106 HDL CPQS
(H-P-04/99)

Name: _____

PLEASE PRINT CLEARLY

Address: _____ Apt.#: _____

City: _____ State/Prov.: _____ Postal Zip/Code: _____

DETACH AND MAIL CARD TODAY!

7	7	7	WORTH TWO FREE BOOKS PLUS A BONUS MYSTERY GIFT!
🍒	🍒	🍒	WORTH TWO FREE BOOKS!
♣	♣	♣	WORTH ONE FREE BOOK!
🔔	🔔	🍒	TRY AGAIN!

The Harlequin Reader Service® — Here's how it works:

Accepting your 2 free books and mystery gift places you under no obligation to buy anything. You may keep the books and gift and return the shipping statement marked "cancel." If you do not cancel, about a month later we'll send you 6 additional novels and bill you just $3.12 each in the U.S., or $3.49 each in Canada, plus 25¢ delivery per book and applicable taxes if any.* That's the complete price and — compared to the cover price of $3.75 in the U.S. and $4.25 in Canada — it's quite a bargain! You may cancel at any time, but if you choose to continue, every month we'll send you 6 more books, which you may either purchase at the discount price or return to us and cancel your subscription.

*Terms and prices subject to change without notice. Sales tax applicable in N.Y. Canadian residents will be charged applicable provincial taxes and GST.

If offer card is missing write to: Harlequin Reader Service, 3010 Walden Ave., P.O. Box 1867, Buffalo, NY 14240-1867

BUSINESS REPLY MAIL
FIRST-CLASS MAIL   PERMIT NO. 717   BUFFALO, NY

POSTAGE WILL BE PAID BY ADDRESSEE

HARLEQUIN READER SERVICE
3010 WALDEN AVE
PO BOX 1867
BUFFALO NY 14240-9952

NO POSTAGE
NECESSARY
IF MAILED
IN THE
UNITED STATES

shampoo and conditioner. It occurred to her she was playing with fire but the warmth coursing through her felt so good she didn't care.

"Goddammit! I did my best to be decent to you," Steve bellowed.

"Oh? You call getting another woman pregnant being decent?" Amy flared.

"I bet you were already sneaking behind my back…"

"Amy sneak?" Jake laughed at him. "She is the most confrontationist woman I know. Sparks and spice and all things nice."

Steve glared furiously at her. "And I was fool enough not to believe Brooke when she told me you just couldn't wait to have it off with him."

"Well, sometimes Brooke does get things right," Amy fired back heedlessly.

"I feel exactly the same way," Jake declared with fervour. "In fact, I can hardly wait for you to leave."

"And you do have Brooke's party to go to," Amy pressed. "Apart from which, I'm sure your wedding will supply more suitable photos and mementos for your future." She lifted her glass in a mock toast. "Happy days!"

Unfortunately there was no champagne left in it to drink.

"Darling…" Jake purred "…let me take that empty glass." He plucked it out of her hand and set it on the table. "Bad luck you didn't get what you came for, Steve," he burbled on as he swept Amy into his embrace. "But as my girl here says, what's gone is gone. And it's well past time you were gone, too. Would you mind letting yourself out?"

"You know what she called you, Carter?" Steve yelled at him, his face twisting in triumphant scorn. "Jake the rake!"

"Well, fair's fair," Jake said, totally unperturbed. He whipped off his T-shirt and spread her hands against his bare chest. "You can do some raking, too, Amy. I'd like that. I'd like that very much." And his voice wasn't a purr anymore. More like the growl of a wolf with his dinner in view.

It should have frightened her. This whole scene was flying out of her control. Yet the fierce yellow blaze in his eyes was mesmerising and his skin had a magnetic pulse that compelled contact.

"You'll regret it," Steve jeered, but the words seemed to come to her through a fog, setting them at an irrelevant distance, and the door slam that followed them was no more than an echo of the throb in her temples.

"Let me rake you as you've never been raked before," Jake murmured, the low throaty sound hitting on some wild primitive chord that leapt in eager response, and his fingers were running through her hair, tilting her head back.

Then it was too late to pull away, even if she'd found the will to do it, because his mouth took possession of hers and she was sucked into a vortex of irresistible sensation from which there was no escape, nor any wish to. The desire to drown in what Jake Carter could do to her was utterly, savagely overwhelming.

CHAPTER ELEVEN

THE sheer passion of that first kiss blew Amy's mind. Conscious thought was bombarded out of existence. An insatiable hunger swept in and took over, demanding to be fed, to be appeased, to be satisfied.

He tasted so good, his tongue tangling with hers in an erotic dance, arousing explosive tingles of excitement across her palate, stirring sensations that streamed through her body which instantly clamoured for a bigger share of what was going on, a more intense share.

Her hands flew up to get out of the way and her breasts fell against the hot heaving wall of his chest, squashing into it, revelling in the rub of silk and firm male flesh and muscle. Her fingers raked his shoulders, his hair, his back, finding purchase to press him closer. She squirmed with pleasure as his hands clawed down her back to close over her buttocks and haul her into a sweet mashing contact with even more prominent and stimulating masculinity.

Clothes formed a frustrating separation.

They got rid of them.

Then everything felt so much more delicious, incredibly sensual, body hair tickling, hard flesh sliding against soft, mouths meshing, moving to taste everything, greedy, greedy, greedy, loving it, relishing it, feeding on each other in a frenzy of wanting, licking, sucking, hands shaping pathways, beating rhythms, wildly pushing for

99

the ultimate feast of co-mingling, yet not wanting to forgo any appetiser along the way.

Exquisite anticipation, pulse racing, an urgent scream shrieking along nerve-endings, craving…and he lifted her up to make the most intimate connection possible and she wound her legs around his hips and welcomed him in, her muscles rippling convulsively, ecstatically as he filled the need.

And they were one—this wonderful man-wolf and the animal-woman he'd taken as his—as he went down on all fours, lowering her with him to some flat furry surface on the floor, and she tightened the grip of her legs around his hips, fearing the emptiness of losing him. But there was no loss. No loss at all.

With the purchase of ground beneath them he drove in deeper… oh, so soul-shakingly deep, the power of him radiating through her, waves and waves of it, building an intensity that rippled through every cell so it felt as though they were coalescing, melting, fusing with the thunder of his need to possess all of her, and she gave herself up to him, surfing the peaks he pushed her to, wallowing voluptuously in the swell of them, urging him on with wild little cries, exulting in the hot panting of his breath on her, the nails digging into her flesh, the pound of his heart, and the sheer incredible glory of this mating.

Even the ending of it felt utterly fulfilling, climactic in every sense, the shudder of his release spilling her into an amazing, floating, supernatural experience where all existence was focused internally and he was there— the warm, vital essence of him—and that part of him would always be part of her from this moment on.

Then his body sank onto hers, covering it in a final claim, imprinting the power, intoxicating her with it, lulling her into a peaceful acceptance of an intimacy which blotted out everything else because this had a life of its own and it was complete unto itself...like a primitive ritual enacted in a different world.

How long she lay in a euphoric daze, Amy had no idea. Somewhere along the line her mate had shifted both of them to lie on their sides, her body scooped against his spoon-fashion, one of his arms around her waist, the other cushioning her head. Gradually her eyes focused on the balcony she was facing and she became conscious of a strange reality.

Her two cane armchairs were sitting out there, along with the coffee table that served her lounge setting. She hadn't put them on the balcony. The glass doors were open and somehow those pieces of furniture had got out there without her knowledge. The table should be right in the centre of the mat in front of the lounge...except she was lying on the mat instead...and Jake Carter was lying right behind her...both of them very, very naked!

The slowly groping activity in Amy's mind stopped right there. A shock screen went up, forbidding any closer examination of how and when and why. A soft breeze was wafting in. It was pleasantly cool, certainly not cold enough to raise goose bumps, yet Amy's skin prickled with a host of them. Jake moved a big muscly leg over her thigh, nuzzled the curve of her shoulder and neck with a soft, seductive mouth, and slid his hand up from her waist to warm her breasts, his palm gently rotating over her highly sensitised skin.

"Getting cold?" he murmured.

"Yes." It was a bare whisper. Her throat had seized up, along with her shocked heart and frozen mind. She felt as paralysed as a rabbit caught in headlights.

"A hot spa bath should do the trick," he said, and before Amy could even begin to get herself into a semblance of proper working order, he'd somehow heaved them both off the floor and was carrying her to the bathroom, and she was staring over his shoulder at the mat where it had all happened.

Well, not quite all.

It had begun near the table. His orange T-shirt was hanging off one of the dining chairs. Her silk wraparound lay in a crumpled heap on the floor between the table and the lounge. A pair of white shorts had been pitched right across the room to droop drunkenly over the television set. She couldn't see what had happened to the sandals he'd been wearing.

Her view was blocked off as Jake moved through the archway and into the bathroom. He sat on the tiled ledge around the Jacuzzi, settled her on his lap and turned on the taps full blast. Amy didn't know where to look. Luckily he started kissing her again so she just closed her eyes and let him do whatever he liked.

Which he was extremely good at.

She certainly had to grant him that.

Though she was equally certain he had taken advantage of her...her susceptibility...to his...his manpower...which was stirring again and her body was riven by an uncontrollable urge to shift to a more amenable position, like sitting astride those two great thighs instead of across them.

As though Jake instinctively knew this was more appropriate, he rearranged her with such slick speed, it seemed like one lovely fluid movement with him sliding right back into the space that wanted him, filling it with a really delicious fullness.

It felt great. Even better when he started drawing her nipples into his mouth, tugging on the distended nubs, setting up a fantastic arc of sensation that zipped from her breasts to the deep inner sharing, driving her awareness of it to a kind of sensual madness that refused to be set aside.

The taps were turned off, the jets of water switched on and they slipped into the bath, still revelling in the erotic intimacy of being locked together. One part of her mind warned Amy she would have to face what she was doing with Jake Carter, but most of it just didn't want to think at all. Feeling was much more seductive and satisfying.

"Warm now?" he asked.

"Mmmh…"

He laughed, a low throaty gurgle coated with deep satisfaction. "Can't hold it in water, sweetheart, but let me tell you I've never had it so good."

She sighed over the inevitability of their connection ending, though she even found pleasure in his shrinking, feeling the relaxation of her inner muscles as the pressure decreased and tantalisingly slipped away. She peered through her lashes at the happy grin on his face and privately admitted she'd never had it so good, either, but she wasn't sure she should echo his words.

He was still Jake the rake.

Still her boss.

Letting him know he'd won first prize on the sexual

front might mess up things even worse than they'd already been messed up. Amy didn't know how to deal with this situation. Another bridge had been burnt and the future was now a lot murkier than it had been before. She pushed herself down to the other end of the bath and tried to get her mind into gear. Some straight thinking might help.

Jake raised his eyebrows at her in teasing inquiry while his eyes danced with the wicked knowledge that she couldn't ignore what they'd just shared.

Then she remembered the heart-sickening frequency of his sharing with other women. What if he told all of them he'd never had it so good? A charming ego-stroke to top everything off? And just in case he forgot their names in the heat of the moment...

"Don't call me sweetheart!"

The words shot out of her mouth with such vehemence, both of them were startled by their passionate protest. Amy was shaken by how violently she recoiled from having joined an easily forgotten queue, and Jake's good humour instantly lost its sparkle, his eyes narrowing, focusing intensely on her. His sudden stillness suggested he was harnessing all his energy to the task of perceiving the problem.

"I don't use that endearment loosely, Amy," he said quietly. "You *are* sweet to my heart. But if you don't like it..."

"I have a name. I'm not one of your passing parade, Jake. I'm your P.A.," she cried. "Just because I've committed the ultimate folly of going to bed with my boss, doesn't turn me into a no-name woman."

"You? Amy Taylor a no-name woman?" He threw

back his head and laughed. "Never in a million years!" A golden star-burst of twinkles lit his eyes. "And you know we didn't go to bed, Amy. You specifically said you weren't going to bed with me and I respected that decision."

Her insides were mush, churning with a million uncertainties, yet being hopelessly tugged by the sheer attraction of the man. Was she sweet to his heart? All she really knew was they'd done it, bed or no bed, and she was in a state of helpless confusion over what it meant or might mean to either of them.

Before she could think of any reply to him, he shook his head at her and offered a wry little smile as he made the pertinent comment, "Neither of us can blame ourselves for spontaneous combustion."

This implied he hadn't planned what happened, any more than she had. An accident of Fate? Or a convenient excuse?

"Was it?" she asked suspiciously.

"What?"

"Spontaneous combustion."

"It felt like that to me." His brow puckered for a thoughtful moment. "I remember I was swinging in with all the support I could think of for your out-of-my-life act, socking it home to your ex, then…yes, I'd definitely have to call it spontaneous combustion. Mind you, the chemistry was always there. No denying it."

Amy had to accept the undeniable truth that she'd played with fire, tempted the devil, and the ensuing conflagration could not be entirely laid at Jake's door. She sighed, letting go the craven wish to dissolve in the bath. There was no escaping what had to be faced.

"So what do we do now?" she asked, looking for some signal from him.

He grinned at her. "I suggest we have dinner. Both of us need re-fuelling."

Pragmatic Jake. One appetite burnt out…might as well get on with feeding another.

Which could then re-ignite the first and… Amy clamped down on that thought. She had to get sex with Jake off her brain. More practical matters needed to be settled.

"Okay," she agreed. "You dry yourself off first and I'll follow."

He eyed her quizzically. "You're not going shy on me, are you, Amy?"

It triggered a nervous laugh. "A bit late for that. I just want the bathroom to myself while I tidy up."

In truth, Amy didn't want to risk tangling physically with Jake, with or without towels. She needed some clear space here to tidy up her responses to him.

"Fair enough," he said and whooshed out of the bath, the massive displacement of water almost causing a tidal wave.

He was a big man. Stark naked, there was a lot of him, all of it impressive. Amy couldn't help staring. In every male sense he was well proportioned, well muscled and most decisively well endowed. Very well indeed. Her vaginal muscles went into spasms of excitement just looking at him, remembering how he'd felt and what he'd done.

It was just as well she was still lying in the bath. Jake didn't even have to apply the art of temptation in the nude. He was *it*. He turned to reach for a towel and his backside scored a perfect ten beyond a shadow of a doubt.

Amy was struck by a powerful insight. Lust was not a male prerogative. Lust could hit a woman like a runaway train. She was left wondering how on earth it could be stopped.

A more urgent question was…did she *want* it to be stopped?

CHAPTER TWELVE

DINNER was good. Jake didn't press anything but food on her. He played the charming host, ready to serve her every whim, encouraging her to try everything he'd brought, pleased when she did, obviously resolved on giving her a breathing space and setting a relaxed mood.

Amy appreciated it. She appreciated the food, too. It seemed to stabilise her stomach and clear her head. Her confusion over the sexual element that had scrambled their relationship, gradually sorted itself out into various straight avenues of thought.

Of course, it helped that Jake was fully clothed again. And she felt…safer, protected…in the jeans and T-shirt she'd planned to wear before Steve's fateful intrusion. Probably her choice of clothes had alerted Jake to her nervous tension and reservations about any further intimate involvement. He was never slow on picking up signals.

Nevertheless, there could be no avoiding a discussion on where they went from here. As they cleared the dishes from the table, transferring them to the kitchen counter, Amy decided it couldn't be postponed any longer. She could only hope Jake would understand her position.

"Coffee on the balcony?" he suggested.

Her gaze zapped to the armchairs and coffee table he must have put outside while she'd been in the shower prior to Steve's arrival. "You thought of that before," she blurted out, flushing with embarrassment as she recollected precisely when she'd noticed their removal to the balcony.

He shrugged. "It seemed a pleasant way to finish off the evening."

She looked him straight in the eye, something she'd had difficulty in doing throughout dinner. "You didn't come here to jump me, did you, Jake?"

"No," he answered unequivocally. His face softened into a warm, whimsical smile. "I do genuinely care about you. I didn't want you to feel alone."

Her heart turned over.

Maybe caring made the difference.

"Besides, jumping isn't my style," he went on. "I'm only interested in mutual desire."

Desire…lust…he'd probably *cared* about all the others, too.

His eyes gleamed their dangerous wolf-yellow. "And it is very mutual, Amy. Don't put other labels on it."

Don't put *love* on it…that was certain.

Mutual desire was not going to lead anywhere good and it was no use wishing it might. Heat raced into her cheeks again as she tried to explain her spontaneous combustion away.

"Jake…it was just a moment in time…because of Steve…and…"

"No." He shook his head at her. "At least be honest, Amy. We're not ships passing in the night. What happened has been building between us for a long time. A progression…"

"But we don't have to choose it," she cried, agitated

by the way he was validating what had been madness on both their parts. "We work together, Jake. Please don't make it impossible for us to keep on working together."

He frowned as though he hadn't taken that factor into consideration.

"I'll make the coffee," she said, scooting off to the kitchen, hoping to keep the counter between them for a while.

Clothes didn't really help, not when he started radiating physical charm and reminding her of the desires they had indulged so...so wildly. If he reached out and touched her, she wasn't sure she could resist touching back. She had the feeling an electric current would sizzle her brain and her body would proceed on its own merry way to meltdown.

To her intense relief, Jake wandered out to the balcony. She stacked the plates and cutlery into the dishwasher as the coffeemaker did its job. The activity covered her inner turmoil as she clung desperately to what was the only sensible resolution to this volatile situation.

It couldn't go on. Couldn't! Jake's idea of a *progression* threw her into a panic. The sex had been good. Amazing. Incredibly marvellous. But it wouldn't stay that way. Moods and feelings were rarely recaptured. Lust did peter out. She had the evidence of Jake's many affairs to demonstrate how quickly it passed.

The article in the women's magazine which still lay in the bottom drawer of her desk came sharply to mind. If she indulged herself in more physical pleasures with Jake Carter, she'd be looking for the exit signs, every minute of every day, not trusting their togetherness to last long. Then how awkward would it be when he started looking for a fresh experience? How destroying it would be!

No, it was wrong for her. It would mess her up even more than she was already messed up. No matter what he said or did, she couldn't allow herself to be tempted. Now was the time to start building a hopeful future for herself, not plunge down a sidetrack to more misery.

The coffeemaker beeped. She filled two mugs, steeled herself for the stand she had to make, then set out to fight the man who was undoubtedly plotting a different scenario. Her hands shook so much the coffee slurped over. She put the mugs on the counter and walked slowly around it, clenching and unclenching her hands. Her chest was so tight, her heart felt as though it was banging against it, stifled for proper room. Nevertheless, she did manage to carry the mugs out and set them on the coffee table without further spillage.

Jake was leaning on the balcony railing, apparently taking in the night view. He didn't turn even though he must have heard her. Having got rid of the mugs from her nervous hands, Amy fidgeted. Sitting down didn't feel right. It was impossible to relax enough to make it look natural. Yet to join Jake at the railing in the semi-darkness...

"Tell me what you want, Amy."

The soft words caught at her heart, turning her doubts and fears into silly trivialities. Jake had moved on to the big picture. He was simply waiting for her to paint in how she saw it.

Without any further hesitation, she stepped over to the railing and took a deep breath of fresh sea air. The wink-

ing myriad of lights around the bay assured her of life
going on in a normal fashion, despite the ups and downs
everyone was subjected to from time to time. It was
normality she needed now.

"I want to keep my job," she said simply.

He didn't move, not even to glance at her. She had
the sense of him being darkly self-contained, waiting and
listening, biding his time until he had what he needed to
work with.

"There's no question of your losing it," he assured
her.

"I want to feel comfortable in it. I need to feel secure
in it," she explained further. "It's my anchor right now.
If you take that away from me..."

"Why on earth would I?"

He sounded genuinely puzzled.

"You could make it too difficult for me to stay."

"You think I'm going to chase you around the office?" he asked, the dry irony in his voice mocking such
a notion. "It's a fool's game, mixing business with pleasure, Amy. Have I ever seemed that much of a fool to
you?"

"No."

"I respect you far too much to press unwanted attention on you anyway."

"I'm sorry. I...maybe I've got this wrong," she
rushed out in an agony of embarrassment. "I shouldn't
have assumed you'd want to..."

"Oh, yes, I want to, Amy. I really would be a fool
not to want to make love with you whenever I can.
Outside of office hours."

He spoke matter-of-factly yet Amy was left in no

doubt he meant every word of it. One taste was not enough for him. He wanted more, and just the thought of him wanting more aroused all the sensitised places in her body that craved the same.

"But I'd hate you to feel...under duress," he added, his voice dropping to a low rasp of distaste.

The choice was hers, he was saying, and she should have felt relieved, except she was so twisted up inside, her mind couldn't dictate anything sensible.

"It has to be freely given," he went on. "As it was tonight." He half turned to her, a lopsided smile curving his mouth. "You did want me, you know. Not because of Steve. You wanted *me*."

Amy was further shaken by the passion creeping through the quiet control he'd maintained. "Any woman would want you, Jake," she blurted out.

"You're not...any...woman." He flashed her a scathing look. "For God's sake, Amy! Do you think it's like that every time I turn around?"

"How would I know?" she flared back at him, losing the sane control she'd tried so hard to hold on to. "You turn around so often..."

"Because once I know it's not going to work I don't string a woman along as a convenient backup while I cheat on the side, as your precious Steve did," he shot at her.

Pain exploded through her. "Fine!" she fired back at him. "Just don't expect me to give repeat performances until you decide it's not working for you anymore. I'd rather choose my own exit, thank you very much."

He straightened up, aggression emanating from him in such strong waves, Amy almost cringed against the railing. Pride stiffened her spine. She was not going to be intimidated. The memory of her mother being cowed by her father flashed into her mind. Jake had that kind of power but she would not give in to it. Never! She would stand up for what was right for her, no matter what the consequences.

Maybe he sensed her fierce challenge. Something wrought a change. The aggression faded. She felt him— the strength of his will—reaching out to her even before he raised a hand in a gesture of appeal.

"It could be something special for both of us, Amy," he said in soft persuasion.

The fire in her died, leaving only the pain. "It *was* special. Please…leave it there," she begged. "I don't want to fight with you, Jake."

He sighed and offered a wry smile. "I don't want to fight with you, either. Nor do I want you to regret tonight."

She had a hazy memory of Steve yelling, *you'll regret it,* and everything within her rebelled against his mean-minded prediction. Besides, *he* had never once given her so much intense pleasure, never once swept her into such an all-encompassing sensual world. That belonged to Jake and she would never forget it…surely a once-in-a-lifetime experience which had exploded from a unique set of circumstances.

"I'll never regret it, Jake. It was something very special," she reiterated, because it was the truth and it was only fair to admit it to him.

His smiled widened, caressing her with his remembered pleasure. "Then you'll keep it as a good memory?"

He was giving in…letting go…

"Yes," she cried in dizzy relief.

"Of course, if you ever want to build on the good memory, you will keep me in mind," he pressed teasingly.

She laughed, the release of tension erupting through her so suddenly she couldn't help but laugh. It was the old Jake back again, the one she was used to handling, and she loved him for giving him back to her.

"I couldn't possibly consider anyone else," she promised him.

"I can rest content with that," he said, sealing the sense of security she'd asked him for. "And just remember, Amy, you're not alone. You do have me to count on."

Unaccountably after the laughter, tears swam into her eyes. "Thank you, Jake," she managed huskily, overcome with a mixture of sweet feelings that were impossible to define.

"It's okay," he assured her, then stepped over, squeezed her shoulder in a comradely fashion, gently pushed her hair aside and dropped a kiss on her forehead. "Goodnight, Amy. Don't you fret now. It's back to work on Monday."

She was swallowing too hard to say anything. He touched her cheek tenderly in a last salute, and she could only watch dumbly as he walked away from her. All the way to the door she felt the tug of him. Her body churned with need, screaming at her to call him back, take him into her bed, have him as long as she could.

But she stayed still, breathlessly still, and listened to the door closing behind him.

"Goodnight," she whispered.

It had been good.

Best that it stayed good.

CHAPTER THIRTEEN

DESPITE Jake's assurances, Amy's nerves were strung tight as she walked down Alfred Street on Monday morning. Resolutions kept pumping through her mind. She was not going to look at Jake and see him naked. She had to focus every bit of her concentration on the job. And act naturally.

Acting naturally was very important. No overt tension, no signs of agitation, no silly slips of the tongue. Think before you speak, Amy recited over and over again. Pretend it's last week. Pretend it's next week. No matter what she felt in the hours ahead of her, it would pass.

Determined not to falter, Amy pushed past the entrance doors to their office building and strode down the foyer to the elevators. "Hi, Kate!" she called to the receptionist, and practised a bright smile.

"Well, that's a happier start to the week," Kate remarked, smiling back. "No Monday blues. Things must have picked up for you."

Had it only been a week since Steve dumped her? Amy felt as though she'd shifted a long way since then. And she had. All the way to Balmoral. Which was absolutely lovely.

"Feeling good," she declared, pressing the Up button with blithe panache. Positive thinking had to help. "Boss in?"

"Up and running."

"How did your weekend go?" Amy asked, wondering if she could make a friend of Kate.

"I Christmas shopped till I dropped," she replied with a mock groan.

Christmas! Barely three weeks away. And she had no one to share it with this year. No one to buy presents for. But that didn't mean she couldn't celebrate it herself, buy a Christmas tree for the apartment and think of different things to do. She was not going to feel depressed. She had her composure in place and she simply couldn't afford to let anything crack it.

The elevators doors opened and Amy stepped in, throwing Kate a cheery wave. "See you later."

The ride in the elevator was mercifully short. Amy carried the power of positive thinking right to Jake's office. Their connecting door was open. She gave a courtesy knock and stepped inside, exuding all the confidence she could muster.

"Good morning," she trilled, smiling so hard her face ached.

Jake was reading a brochure on planes, chair leaning back, feet up on the desk. He looked over it, cocked an eyebrow at her and said, "The top of the morning to you, too."

"Start with the mail?" she asked.

"I've already looked at the E-mail messages. Go and read the inbox and get up to date. We'll deal with the Erikson inquiry first. And check the diary, Amy. We'll have to set up a meeting with him."

"Right!"

She was almost out of his office when he raised his voice in command.

"Hold it!"

Amy's heart jumped and pitter-pattered all around her chest. She held on to the door and popped her head around it. "Something else?" she inquired.

Jake had swung his feet off the desk and was leaning forward, beetling a frown at her. "You're wearing black. Didn't I specifically tell you my P.A. was not to wear black?"

It was true. He had. "I forgot," she said. Which was also true.

"Black does not fit our image, Amy," he said sternly. "Black is safe. Black is neutral..."

Which was precisely why she had chosen it this morning, having dithered through her entire wardrobe.

He wagged a finger at her. "Black is not to be worn again."

"Right!" she agreed.

"Just as well we don't have any important client meetings today," he muttered, then shot her a sharp look. "You're not in a black mood, are you?"

"No!" she denied swiftly.

"Good!" His expression brightened. The familiar teasing twinkled into his eyes as he lifted his feet back on the desk. "You can wear red anytime you like. You look stunning in red."

He picked up the brochure again and Amy skipped out to start work, her heart dancing instead of pitter-pattering. Everything was normal. Everything was fine. Jake was as good as his word. Life could go on as it had before.

Almost.

Amy found the to-and-fro between them wasn't quite

as easy as the day wore on. Not that she could lay any fault at Jake's door. Not once did he do or say anything to discomfort her along intimate lines. The problem was all hers.

When Jake bent over to pick up some papers he'd dropped, and the taut contours of his backside were clearly outlined, his trousers just disappeared and she could see him stepping out of the bath in all his natural glory. When he sat down and crossed his legs, the bulge of his powerful thighs vividly reminded her of their strong, bouncy support when she'd sat astride them. His mouth generated quite a few unsettling moments, too. She hoped Jake didn't notice these little distractions.

Lust, she decided, was not a runaway train. It was more like a guerilla soldier who could creep up and capture you before you even knew he was coming. But the memories of that *special* time with Jake were still very fresh, she told herself. Given a few days, they wouldn't leap to the forefront of her mind quite so much.

As it turned out, by the end of the week, Amy was really enjoying her job again, feeling a sense of achievement in meeting the challenges Jake regularly tossed at her, countering his bouts of teasing with the occasional smart quip, helping with the deals he set up and made for their clients. Best of all, without her old hackles rising all the time, she was open-minded enough to realise Jake truly did value and appreciate her contribution to his business.

He showed it in many ways, generous with compliments if what she'd done warranted them, giving consideration to her opinions and impressions of clients, readily taking suggestions if he thought them effective.

She was also more acutely aware of the close rapport they shared, where just a look conveyed a message which was instantly understood. Two years of familiarity did build that kind of knowledge of each other, she reasoned, yet she was beginning to feel she was more attuned to Jake's way of thinking than she'd ever been to Steve's, so the longevity of a relationship did not necessarily count.

As she left the office on Friday, she was wishing there was no weekend and it would be work as usual tomorrow. Which showed her she was becoming too dependent on Jake's company. Get a life, she sternly told herself.

On Saturday she canvassed several gyms between Balmoral and Milsons Point to see what equipment and classes they offered, comparing their fees, chatting to instructors, appraising their clienteles. She did some research on dance schools, as well, having always fancied learning tap-dancing. Wait for classes to be resumed in the new year, she was advised.

Saturday night proved difficult. It didn't matter what she tried to do, her mind kept wandering to Jake. She couldn't imagine him sitting at home by himself. He'd be involved in some social activity—a party, a date— and one or more women would be enjoying his charm and attention, beautiful sexy women who wouldn't say no to an experience with Jake Carter.

Envy frayed any peace of mind over her decision to cut any further intimate involvement with him. But it was the right decision, she insisted to herself. At least she was saved from the bitterness of becoming his ex-lover when he started favouring someone else. And her job was safe. No risk of a nasty blow-up there. But "the good memory" lingered with her a long time when she finally took herself off to bed.

She spent Sunday on the beach, determined to relax and enjoy what she had within easy reach. It passed the time pleasantly. She succeeded in pushing Jake to the edge of her mind for most of the day. On Monday morning, however, her hand automatically reached for the scarlet linen shift. She told herself it was stupid to want to look "stunning" for him, but she wore it anyway.

"Ah!" he said when she walked into his office to greet him. It was a very appreciative "Ah!" and the wolfish gleam in his eyes as he looked her up and down put a zing in her soul.

"Image," she said pertly. "We're meeting with Erikson today."

"Of course," he said and grinned at her.

She felt ridiculously happy all day.

The buoyant mood continued for most of the week.

The first niggle of worry came on Friday.

She'd finished the monthly course of contraceptive pills she'd been taking for years and her cycle always worked with clocklike regularity. Her period should have started today. So why hadn't it?

Her mind kept zinging to the night she'd forgotten to take a pill, but she'd taken two the next day to make up for it. Though it was actually the next night—not the morning or the day—when she'd discovered the error and taken double the dose. One missed night. It wouldn't matter normally. She had doubled up before, when she'd accidentally missed one over the years, and nothing had gone wrong.

But this time…this time…

Impossible to forget which night it was…she and Jake losing themselves in spontaneous combustion…and the deep, inner sense of mingling…melding inextricably.

Had their mating…such a terribly evocative word—borne fruit?

It was a nerve-shattering thought. Amy kept pushing it away. It would be the worst irony in the world if she'd fallen pregnant, just when she was trying to get her life in reasonable order after her long-term partner had taken off because he'd got another woman pregnant. Not that she wanted Steve back. That was finished. But Jake…as the father…it didn't bear thinking about.

Her cycle was messed up a day. That was all it was. Any minute it could correct itself. Tomorrow she'd be laughing about this silly worrying. One missed pill…it was nothing in the big picture. Her body wouldn't play such a dirty trick on her when she'd been protecting it against such a consequence for years.

Saturday brought her no relief. By Sunday afternoon Amy was in full panic. She bought a pregnancy test kit from a twenty-four-hour pharmacy. She couldn't bear the uncertainty.

The uncertainty ended on Monday morning.

It didn't matter how much she wanted to disbelieve the results of the test, two deadly pink lines were looking her in the face, not changing to anything else, and according to the instructions with the test kit, this meant she was pregnant. She checked the instructions again and again. No mistake. Pink was positive.

Just maybe, she thought frantically, the kit was faulty. Best see a doctor. Get a blood test. She looked through the telephone directory, found a medical centre at Mosman along the route she drove to work, then considered what lie she could tell to cover her late arrival at the office.

Impossible to say she needed to see a doctor. Jake would ask why. Jake wouldn't leave it alone until he found out. A flat tyre on her car, she decided. It could happen to anyone.

The visit to the doctor was a nightmare. Yes, missing a pill at a critical time could result in pregnancy. Test kits were usually reliable but a blood test would give absolute confirmation. Amy watched the needle going in and almost fainted as the blood started filling up the tube, blood that was going to tell her the awful truth. A baby! She closed her eyes. No, no, no, she begged. Having a baby—Jake's baby—made life too impossible.

She'd have the results in twenty-four hours, the doctor said. All she had to do was telephone the surgery and ask for them. She checked her watch. Nine-thirty. Twenty-four more hours of hell to get through, a third of those hours with the man who'd done this to her.

Not intentionally.

Though he should have used protection...should at least have asked her if she was protected. In which case she would have said yes, so there was no point in blaming him. Nevertheless, she might have remembered to take the wretched pill if he'd asked. Spontaneous combustion might be a very special experience but the "good memory" was swiftly gathering a mountain of savage regrets.

Jake, the rake... How would he react to being told he'd sown one too many oats? With his P.A., no less.

But she didn't have to face that yet.

Not yet.

Twenty-four hours.

Amy didn't know how she got through the day with Jake. He asked about the flat tyre and she blathered on about it, excusing the time away from the office. She was aware of him frowning at her several times. It was almost time for her to leave when he asked, "Is something wrong, Amy?" and her glazed eyes cleared enough to see he was observing her very keenly.

Would their child have those wolf eyes?

Her stomach cramped.

"No," she forced out. "Everything's fine." *Except I'm probably pregnant.*

"You haven't been with me, today," he remarked testingly.

"Sorry. I have been a bit scatter-brained. Christmas coming on..."

"Planning anything special?"

The excuse had popped into her mind but she was totally blank about it and had to grope for a reply. "No. Not really. Just...well, I guess I was thinking about the family I don't have. Kate Bradley was saying she'd shopped till she dropped and..." Amy shrugged, having run out of ideas to explain herself. "At least I'm saved that hassle."

Christmas...celebrating the birth of a child...

Dear God! Please don't do this to me.

"Uh-huh," Jake murmured noncommittally. "Not a good thing, spending Christmas alone. No fun in all. I'll speak to my sister about it."

"What?" Amy didn't understand what his sister had to do with it.

"Leave it to me," he said and went back into his office.

Amy shook her head in bewilderment. She simply wasn't in tune with Jake's thought processes today. But at least he'd stopped questioning her and she wasn't about to chase after him and invite more probing into her own thought processes, which were hopelessly scrambled by the waiting to know.

The next morning, she wasn't free of Jake's presence until ten-thirty. Almost sick with apprehension, she pounced on the telephone and called the surgery, all the while watching the door she'd closed between Jake's office and hers, desperately willing it to stay closed. Which it did, thankfully, because the news she received, although expected, still came as a shock.

No doubt about it anymore.

She *was* pregnant.

To Jake Carter.

And she had no idea in the wide world what to do about it.

An abortion?

Instant recoil.

Tell Jake.

No, she wasn't ready for that. She needed time to armour herself against...whatever she had to armour herself against.

An unworthy thought flashed through her mind. Steve's blonde had used her pregnancy to pull him into marriage. Would Jake...

No, Amy fiercely decided. She couldn't—wouldn't—

go down that road. Marriage could be a trap, as she well knew, and using a baby to seal the trap would be a terrible thing to do to all three of them. Jake wasn't the marrying kind. He was the perennial bumblebee flitting from flower to flower.

He'd probably be appalled at the prospect of father-hood being thrust upon him...a long-term relationship he couldn't get out of. Unless she had an abortion. Would he ask it of her?

She'd hate him if he did.

She remembered the lovely, natural way he'd handled his baby nephew, Joshua. Surely, with his own child...

The telephone rang.

Amy picked up the receiver, struggling to get her wits together to handle a work-related call.

"Good morning..."

"Amy, is that you? Amy Taylor?" an eager female voice she didn't recognise broke in.

"Yes..."

"Good! It's Ruth Powell here, Jake's sister."

"Oh?" The coincidence of having just been thinking of Ruth's son dazed Amy for a moment. "How can I help you?"

"We'd all love you to come for Christmas Day, Amy. It's at my house this year. Well, mine and Martin's, nat-urally. The rest of the family will be here and they're dying to meet you. Jake said you didn't have family of your own to go to, so how about joining us? It'll be such fun!"

This was rattled out at such high speed, Amy was slow to take it in. "It's...very nice of you, Ruth..."

"Please say you can. It's no trouble, I promise you.

We'll have food enough for an army. Mum's bringing the turkey and my sisters-in-law are providing the ham and the pudding, and Jake, of course, is in charge of the drinks. We've told him, nothing but the best French champagne…''

Which had probably contributed to the mess she was in, Amy thought miserably.

"So you see," Ruth went on, "we'll have the best time. All the festive stuff has been thought of and you must see my tree. It's Joshua's first Christmas and Martin and I bought the most splendid tree you can imagine. Fabulous decorations. Please say you'll come, Amy."

She never had got around to buying a tree. Too much else on her mind. Jake's baby. And this was his family—her baby's family—inviting her to meet them. Suddenly it felt important to do so, to see Jake in action with his family, to see him with children…

"Thank you, Ruth. It's such a kind thought…"

"You'll come?" she cried excitedly.

"Yes. I'd like to."

"Great! Jake will pick you up at…"

"No, please, I don't want that. He should be with you."

"He won't mind."

"Ruth, *I'd* mind." She could cope with him in office hours. Outside of them…her stomach quivered. "I'd rather come and go by myself," she stated firmly.

Ruth laughed. "Still keeping him in line. Good for you, Amy! Does eleven o'clock Christmas morning suit you?"

"Yes. Where do you live?"

The address was given and the call ended, Ruth sounding triumphantly satisfied with the arrangements.

It was really Jake's doing, Amy realised, remembering how he'd questioned her about Christmas yesterday.

He didn't like the idea of her being alone.

The irony was the last time he'd acted to save her from being alone, he'd left her pregnant, ensuring she wouldn't be alone in the future.

But where was he going to stand in her future?

He did care about her.

But how much? ...How much?

Christmas...

Maybe that would be the day she'd find out.

CHAPTER FOURTEEN

CHRISTMAS day with the Carter family was happy chaos. From the moment Amy arrived at the Powell home, Ruth linked her arm with hers in warm welcome and whizzed her into a wonderfully large family room which opened out onto a lovely patio and pool garden area. People were scattered everywhere and introductions were very informal.

"Amy, this is my dad, trying to clear the room of wrapping paper."

"Hi, Amy!" An elderly version of Jake grinned at her over the mountain of brilliantly printed Christmas gift wreckage he held in his arms. "I'm sick of wading through this stuff. Might stub my toe on something."

She grinned back. "I can see it might be a problem. Nice to meet you, Mr. Carter."

"And this is our tree," Ruth went on proudly, not giving Amy time to get into conversation. It didn't really seem expected. Which was totally unlike any visitor's encounter with *her* father, who would have demanded full and absolute attention.

The tree was, indeed, fabulous—three metres tall, at least, towering up towards the cathedral ceiling, a green fir draped in red and purple and silver ornaments and hundreds of fairy lights.

Amy was swept into the adjoining kitchen where two women were gathered around an island bench loaded with festive food. "Grace, Tess, here she is. These two busy bodies are my sisters-in-law, Amy."

She managed a "Hi!" before being interrupted.

"At last!" Grace, a plump and very pretty brunette exclaimed, brown eyes twinkling triumphant delight. "You're making our day, Amy. We can really henpeck Jake about you now."

"Pardon?" The word tripped out as alarm shot through Amy. She didn't want to be a target of teasing, no matter how good-natured it was. The situation was too serious for her to respond light-heartedly.

Tess laughed. She was a honey-blonde and obviously pregnant, making Amy even more conscious of her own condition. "Don't worry, Amy," she was quick to assure. "We won't embarrass you. It's just that our brother-in-law is such a slippery customer when it comes to women, it's nice to hang one on him."

"I am only his P.A.," she reminded them.

"Don't say *only*," Ruth instantly expostulated. "We think you're marvellous. The only constant female in Jake's life, apart from his family."

"And he cared enough to want you here," Grace put in.

"Which proves he *can* care," Tess declared. "We were beginning to doubt he was capable of it. You're the only one he's ever wanted to share his Christmas with, Amy."

"Well, we do share a lot of days," Amy explained, trying to hide the flutter of hope in her heart. "I guess he thought this was just another."

"Nope. It's definitely caring," Grace insisted.

"Trust, too," Tess said decisively. "You've given us

hope for him, Amy. He actually trusts you to survive meeting his family. Obviously a woman of strength."

Amy smiled at their free flow of zany humour. "Are you so formidable?"

"Dreadful en masse," Ruth said, rolling her eyes to express the burden of belonging to them. "Loud and competitive and opinionated and everyone tells horrible stories. You'd better come and meet the rest so you can sort them out."

Ruth's husband, Martin, Jake and his two older brothers, Adam and Nathan, were all in the pool, playing water games with five children. "Hannah's the eldest at ten. Olivia's eight. Tom's seven. Mitch is four and Ashleigh's three," Ruth rattled out. "It's a rule in this family that everyone has to learn to swim before they walk."

They all yelled out, "Happy Christmas!" and Amy was struck by their happiness and harmony as they continued their fun. Jake was holding a big plastic ball, ready to throw, and the cries of "Me, Uncle Jake, me!" rang with excitement and pleasure.

She would have liked to stop and watch him frolicking with his nieces and nephews but Ruth steered her to where an elderly woman sat in the shade of a vine-covered pergola, nursing a wide awake Joshua on her lap. "Mum, this is Jake's Amy," she announced.

"Ruth, do try to introduce people properly," her mother chided, and Amy instantly had a flash of Jake saying, "Mum does her best to rule over us all."

"Amy Taylor, please meet Elizabeth Rose Carter," Ruth trotted out in mock obedience.

Her mother sighed. She was still a striking woman,

however old she was. A lovely mass of white wavy hair framed a face very like Ruth's, but her brown eyes were more reserved than openly welcoming.

"It's very kind of you all to include me in your family Christmas, Mrs. Carter," Amy said, aware she was being given a keen scrutiny by Jake's mother during this mother-daughter exchange. "It's a great pleasure to meet you."

"And you, my dear," came the dignified reply. "Jake has spoken so much about you."

"I enjoy working with him," was the only comment Amy could think of.

It was rather disconcerting being measured against whatever Jake had said about her, and being visually measured from head to toe, as well. It was silly to feel self-conscious in her white pantsuit since the other women wore similar casual clothes, but she suddenly wished she'd worn a loose shirt instead of the figure-moulding halter top. *I might be pregnant to him but I'm not a brazen hussy out to trap your son,* she found herself thinking.

"I understand you have no close relatives," Elizabeth Carter remarked questioningly, making Amy feel like a reject of the human race.

"My parents emigrated from England and my brothers now live overseas," she answered. "This kind of gathering is quite remarkable to me. You're very lucky, Mrs. Carter."

"Yes, I suppose I am. Though I tend to think one makes one's own luck. I did bring my children up to value the close bonds of family."

"Then they were very fortunate in having you as their mother."

"What of your own mother, Amy?"

"She died when I was sixteen."

"How sad. A girl needs her mother. So easy to go off the rails without good advice and support."

"I suppose so," Amy said noncommittally, feeling she was being dissected and found wanting. No solid family background. No wise maternal guidance in her life.

"Mum, do you think it's kind to ram that stuff down Amy's throat on today of all days?" Ruth demanded in exasperation.

"Amy!"

Jake's shout saved the awkward moment. They all looked to see what he wanted. He'd hauled himself out of the pool and was striding towards them, rubbing himself vigorously with a towel. Amy's heart caught in her throat. He was so...vital...and stunningly male.

She forced her gaze to stay fixed on his face as he neared them. The rest of his anatomy held too many pitfalls to her peace of mind. Not that she had any peace of mind, but her knees suddenly felt very shaky and if there was ever a time to appear strong it was now, especially in front of his mother's critical eye.

"Sorry I wasn't out of the pool to greet you when you arrived," he said, his smile aimed exclusively at her, a smile that tingled through her bloodstream and made her feel light-headed.

"No need to apologise. Ruth is looking after me," she said, struggling to be sensible. "Go back if you like. I don't want to interrupt the game."

He shook his head. "You look great in that white outfit. Why haven't I seen you in white before?"

"You would have said it's a neutral, not fitting our image," she said dryly.

He grinned, the yellow wolfish gleam lighting his eyes. "Definitely a positive. Give me five minutes to get dressed and I'll be at your side to protect you from the hordes."

"Well, if you're going to poke your nose in, I'm taking Amy back to the kitchen so we women can get some chat in first," Ruth informed him archly.

He laughed. "I can feel the knives in my back. Take no notice of them, Amy. The women in this family have mean, vicious hearts."

"Oh, you..." Ruth tried to cuff him, but he ducked out of reach and was off, still laughing.

"Are you still okay with Joshua, Mum?" Ruth asked.

"Yes, dear." The dark eyes pinned Amy purposefully. "Perhaps we'll have time to converse later."

"I'm sure we will," she answered, forcing a smile she didn't feel. The impression was too strong that Elizabeth Rose Carter did not consider her a suitable person to be the one woman her youngest son chose to share Christmas with his family, let alone be the mother of his child.

It hurt.

And the natural acceptance given her by all the others as the day wore on, didn't quite overlay that initial hurt. It preyed on her mind more and more as she watched the Carter family in action over the long and highly festive Christmas luncheon.

They connected so easily and they had no fear of saying anything they liked to each other. There was no tension. Laughter rippled around the table. Children were lovingly indulged. Good-natured arguments broke out and became quite boisterous but there wasn't a trace of acrimony, merely a lively exchange of opinions accompanied by witty teasing. It was interesting, amusing, and most of all, happy.

Jake didn't allow her to be simply an observer. Neither did his siblings nor their partners. It seemed everyone was keen to draw her into being one of them, inviting her participation, wanting it, enjoying it. Occasionally Jake's father would stir the pot with provocative remarks, then sit back, his amber eyes twinkling like Jake's as comments bounced around the table.

They knew how to have fun, this family. To Amy it was a revelation of how a family could be, given a kindly and encouraging hand at the helm. She wished her baby could know this, know it from the very beginning…to grow up without fear, with an unshakable sense of belonging to a loving circle. Maybe she was idealising it, but the contrast from what she'd come from was so great, it all seemed perfect to her.

The rapport she shared with Jake was heightened in this company. There were times when their eyes met, the understanding felt so intimate she was sure she could tell him she was pregnant and it wouldn't cause any problem between them. He would want his child. He would love it. Family was natural to him.

Then she would catch his mother watching them and knew there was no easy solution to her situation. Elizabeth Carter did not approve of her. Besides, the sense of intimacy was an illusion, generated by the special harmony of a happy Christmas day. Jake might care for her and trust her. It didn't mean he would want to be bound to her through their child.

She was his P.A.

He wasn't in love with her.

He probably wasn't the type to fall in love since he'd never brought any other woman to a family Christmas. Brief affairs was his style when it came to women. She probably wouldn't be here if she was still one of his "brief" affairs. He undoubtedly thought she was *safe*, not expecting anything of him.

After the feast had been devoured to everyone's satisfaction, they drifted out to the patio. Nathan had set up a badminton net beside the pool, and the two older brothers challenged Jake and Ruth to a game. The rest of the family took up spectator positions, ready to barrack for their team. The children sat around the pool, making up their own competition about diving in to retrieve the shuttlecock should it be hit into the water. Elizabeth Carter invited Amy to sit with her under the pergola.

Here comes *the conversation,* Amy thought, and wondered why Jake's mother was bothering. Didn't she know her own son?

"I hope you've been enjoying yourself," she started.

"Immensely," Amy returned with a smile.

"This badminton match is something of a tradition. Jake started it years ago. They'll play on for a while. It's the best of five games."

"Closely fought, I'd imagine."

She actually unbent enough to laugh. "Very. And

they use outrageous tactics. Which is why their father has to umpire.''

"But all done in the spirit of fun, I'm sure," Amy commented.

"Oh, yes." The amusement faded into a shrewd look. "Though life isn't all fun. I've found it's a lot less complicated if one follows a straight path."

"How do you mean?" Amy prompted, thinking they might as well get to the meat of this talk.

"Well, as I understand it from Jake," she started tentatively, "You've been…attached…to a relationship for many years."

"Most people do get attached," Amy said dryly. Not counting Jake, she could have added even more dryly.

Elizabeth Carter gathered herself to spit out what was on her mind. "I must say I don't hold with this modern custom of moving in together," she plunged in, her expression implying she was giving Amy the benefit of her wisdom. "I don't think it does anyone any good in the long run. No clear-cut commitment to a shared future. No emotional security. It's not the right way to go, Amy. Your mother would have told you that," she declared with confidence.

"You didn't know my mother, Mrs. Carter," Amy said quietly. "Nor what she suffered in her marriage. What we all suffered. You may see marriage as a safe haven where people can grow happily. It's not always so."

Silence.

Amy watched the badminton game, her stomach churning over the judgement Jake's mother had made on her—a loose-living woman without commitment. It wasn't fair. It wasn't right. And her defences were very brittle today. She didn't need this. She needed...support.

"I'm sorry. I can only assume your mother made a bad character judgement in her husband," came the gentle rejoinder.

The criticism hit Amy on the raw. One didn't have a clear-minded choice over everything. She hadn't chosen to get pregnant. Especially to a man who didn't love her!

"Perhaps you'd like to give me a reading of Jake's character, Mrs. Carter." Amy swung a hard gaze on her, giving no quarter. "From where I've sat over the past two years, he's a rake with women. A very good boss, a very charming man, but not someone I'd trust to make me happy in the long run, as you so succinctly put it. His turnover rate hardly makes him a good choice, does it? Or do you see it differently?"

The recoil of shock was written all over Elizabeth Carter's face. Being hit by a such a direct and pertinent challenge had certainly not been anticipated. Do her good, Amy thought grimly. Stop her from thinking her youngest son was a glittering prize any woman would love to snatch.

Shock was followed by bewilderment. "Why did you come here today, Amy?"

"I wanted to see what Jake's family is like," she answered bluntly. "It can tell you a lot about a person."

"Then you must understand Jake is looking for the complement to what we have here. He'll keep on looking for it because he won't settle for anything less."

Amy gave her an ironic look. "He's been looking a long time, Mrs. Carter, without success. I may have *moved in* with a man but at least I was constant for five years, which I'm sure Jake told you, and it was my partner's infidelity that broke up the relationship. Infidelity does not appeal to me.''

She frowned. ''I did not mean to offend you, Amy.''

In that case, tact certainly wasn't her strong point, Amy thought.

The frown deepened. ''I know Jake wouldn't cheat on anyone. It isn't in his nature.''

He'd said as much himself, on the balcony after…but that didn't mean he'd stay with one woman for the rest of his life. And Amy suddenly realised it was what she'd want of him…a commitment to her and their child…and it wouldn't happen…so to tell him she was pregnant would almost certainly result in an intolerable situation for both of them. It wouldn't be happy families. It would be emotional hell.

''Don't worry, Mrs. Carter,'' she said ruefully. ''I will not embroil your son in a relationship you wouldn't like.''

''Amy…'' She shook her head in distress. ''Oh, dear… I just wanted to help. I know you've been hurt. Sometimes people just don't see straight and they keep repeating their mistakes instead of learning from them. Moving in together is so…so messy.''

So is divorce, Amy thought, but she held her tongue. The couples in the Carter family looked far too solid for her to make that sour comment.

''I have no intention of moving in with your son,'' she stated flatly. ''I work for Jake. We get on well. This invitation to join you for Christmas was a kindness on his part. It's unnecessary to make more of it than that, believe me.''

And I won't intrude again.

"Jake is kind," his mother said, as though preparing to build a case for her son's *good* character.

"Yes, he is," Amy agreed.

"Underneath all his wild ways, he has a heart of gold. He wouldn't hurt anyone. He goes out of his way not to hurt anyone.''

Amy sighed. "You don't have to defend him to me, Mrs. Carter. I guess I don't like being put in a position where I'm pushed to defend myself. Shall we leave it at that?''

She knew she sounded hard, but she was in a hard place and Jake's mother hadn't made it any easier. Not that anything would, she thought despairingly.

Elizabeth Carter was clearly upset by this outcome. "I'm sorry..." she began again.

"It's okay," Amy rushed out dismissively, wanting the conversation dropped. She couldn't bear it on top of everything else. "Let's just watch the match through and then I'll go.''

"Jake won't want you to go.''

"I make my own decisions, Mrs. Carter.''

She had for a long time. A very long time. Starting when she'd decided independence was the only way to survive intact in her father's household, not to care, not to want, not to need what she didn't have. And now she looked out over Jake's family, feeling like a disembodied outsider, watching a magic circle she could never hope to join. Not freely.

Her baby might be a passport to it in a limited sense—

Jake was kind—but that kindness could be a terrible cruelty, too—to be given a taste while not truly belonging. The only way she and their child could properly belong would be if Jake were her husband, and she couldn't trap him into marriage like that. Marriage should not be a trap. For anyone.

It hurt to watch him. She tried to move her attention to the others but her gaze kept being drawn back to him…the father of her child…the accidental father…unaware that part of him was growing inside her. Was it right not to tell him? Was it best, in the long run, to just disappear from his life?

She didn't know.

She felt as though she didn't know anything anymore.

She was in chaos. It wasn't the happy chaos of a Carter family Christmas. It was the dark chaos that came with the constant beating of uncertainties.

Finally the game was over, Adam and Nathan conceding victory to Jake and Ruth, and Jake was coming for her, wanting her to play.

And she had to find an answer.

CHAPTER FIFTEEN

"WINNER'S choice now," Jake crowed. "Amy and I challenge Ruth and Martin."

"You can have it, boyo," the oldest brother, Nathan, groaned. "I'm for a long cool drink."

"Me, too," Adam agreed. "Preferably in the pool."

"Ah, the frailties of age," Jake teased.

"You'll get yours," Nathan retorted. "Martin will wipe you off the court."

"Huh! You don't know my Amy."

My Amy...and the glorious grin he aimed at her...she couldn't take any more turmoil.

"Not me, Jake," she quickly protested. "Take Grace as your partner. I really must be going now." She stood up, preparing to make her farewells.

"Going?" He looked incredulous.

"It's been a wonderful day..."

"It's not over yet," he argued. "We light up the barbecue at about seven and..."

"I'm sorry. I can't stay."

"Why not?" Ruth demanded, getting in on the act. "We need you to balance up the party, Amy."

She forced a smile. "The truth is I have a raging headache. Too much champagne over lunch, I guess. Please don't mind."

Elizabeth Carter leapt up from her chair. "You should have said, Amy. I'll get you some pills to take."

"You could lie down for a while," Ruth suggested.

"No, please..." Amy reached out to stay Jake's mother, unaware her eyes filled with anguished appeal. "Just let me go. All right?"

The older woman hesitated, then blurted out, "I'm so sorry..."

"For what, Mum?" Jake asked sharply.

"That I'm not up to more fun and games," Amy hastily explained. She forced another smile. "I'd like to say my goodbyes, Jake."

He searched her eyes, obviously sensing something wrong beyond the headache. However, much to Amy's intense relief, he decided not to press the point. "You're the boss today," he said with his quirky smile. "Mum, would you mind getting the headache tablets for Amy to take before she goes?"

"Of course, dear."

"Can't have you driving in pain," he said, then raised his voice. "Hey, everyone! Amy has to leave now so come and wish her well."

They all bunched around, shaking hands, kissing her cheek, saying what a pleasure it was to have met her. It passed in a blur to Amy. She hoped she made suitable responses. Jake's mother handed her a glass of water and two pills. She took them. The raging headache was very real. The crowd around her receded. So did the noise. Finally, there was only Jake who took the glass from her, set it down on a table, then wrapped her arm around his.

"Are you sure you're fit to drive, Amy?" he asked in concern as he walked her into the house.

It was all she could do not to tremble at his touch, his

nearness. He didn't realise the effect he was having on her, the sheer torture of being so closely linked, yet impossibly far from what she wanted of him. "I'll be fine," she insisted huskily.

He paused her in the family room. "I'll sit with you for a while if you like. Some quiet time won't go amiss."

"No. I don't want to be a trouble." It was hard to keep a frantic note out of her voice. She broke away from him to pick up her handbag which she'd left on a chair by the Christmas tree.

Christmas...peace, hope and goodwill...it was a joke... a wickedly painful black joke!

"It's no trouble," Jake assured her.

"I'll be fine," she insisted more firmly, and having collected her bag, she headed for the foyer, every step driven by the need to get away from the torment he stirred.

He followed. "Amy, did Mum say anything to upset you?" Urgent concern in his voice now.

"Why should she?" she flipped back.

"Because my mother has a habit of thinking she knows best," he grated out.

"Most parents do." *Except me,* Amy thought, in helpless panic. Here she was, a parent in the making, with no idea what was best.

"You're not answering my question," Jake persisted.

"It doesn't matter."

He halted her by stepping in front of her, right in the centre of the foyer which served the front door. "*You* matter," he said with quiet force. "You matter to *me.*"

Do I?...Do I?

The words pounded through her mind as she lifted her head to search his eyes for how much she mattered to him. Golden eyes, burning fiercely. But what did it mean?

She didn't see him lift his hand. Her cheek quivered under its tender touch, a touch that was only there fleetingly, because fingers were suddenly raking through her hair and his head bent closer and his mouth claimed hers.

Amy completely lost track of what happened after that. The pain in her head was pushed to some far perimeter, her mind filling up with a host of clamouring needs, every one of them chorusing yes to the connection being forged…yes, to the sweet caress of his lips, yes to the seductive slide of his tongue, yes, yes, yes, to the passionate plunder that followed, a wildly exhilarating, intensely evocative reminder of sensations she'd known before with this man…only this man.

She wasn't aware of moving her body to meet his, of clinging to him, of basking in the heat he generated, the strength emanating from him, surrounding her, cocooning her in a place that felt safe and right. Her whole being was swimming in a sea of bliss, feeling—knowing on some deep subconscious level—this was the answer, the answer to everything.

"Uh-oh…"

Ruth's voice…intruding, jarring.

"…Slice of Christmas cake for Amy… I'll just leave it here."

The pain in Amy's head crashed through the wall of sensation that had held it at bay. The realisation of what she was doing—what Jake was doing—exploded through her mind. This physical compulsion...sexual attraction...*didn't answer anything!*

She tore her mouth from his. Her hands were buried in his hair. Her body was plastered against his, his arms, hands, ensuring she was pressed into maximum, intimate contact, and she'd not only allowed it, she was actively *clinging,* as though he was the only rock that could save her from going under.

Clinging...like's Steve's blonde...for whom she'd felt contempt.

Such a wretched lack of understanding on her part.

Yet she was appalled at her own weakness.

"It's the same," Jake murmured near her ear, his voice furred with satisfaction.

She jerked her head back. Her hands scrambled out of his hair to push at his shoulders, frantic to make some space between them. "You shouldn't have done this. You agreed!" she cried, her eyes meeting his in agitated, anguished accusation.

"It *is* out of office hours," he reminded her in mitigation of the offence. His mouth—his damnably mesmerising mouth—curved into a soft, sensual smile. "And I'd have to confess the temptation to refresh the memory got the better of me."

The memory...still physically surging between them. Flustered by her own complicity in reviving it, Amy broke his embrace, her hands fluttering wildly over his chest as she forced a step back from him, her eyes begging for release.

"You took advantage." Blaming him didn't excuse herself, but she had not invited this. He couldn't say she had.

"Mmh..." He was not the least bit abashed. The smile still lingered on his lips and the molten gold in his eyes remained warm, twinkling with the pleasure of a desire fulfilled. "Look up, Amy."

"What?" She *was* looking up, her gaze trained directly on his, desperately seeking the heart of this man.

"Right above your head is a bunch of mistletoe hanging from the light fitting."

She looked up. There it was, just as he said.

"A man's entitled to kiss a woman standing underneath the mistletoe on Christmas day."

Fun, she thought despairingly. He was having his wicked way with her, out of office hours, just because he wanted to. Never mind how she felt or what it would do to her. Jake, the rake, couldn't resist an opportunity to satisfy himself. Fury swept through her, a fury fed by fear and frustration.

"You deliberately stopped me here," she hurled at him, her hands dropping from all contact from him, curling into fists, her whole body bristling with fierce aggression. How dare he touch her *in fun!* It was monstrous, without care or conscience.

He frowned, perceiving her sense of violation and not liking it. "I'm simply letting you know there's no reason to be fussed by it, Amy."

Fussed! It was the most contemptible word he could have used, making light of what he'd done when it wasn't light at all. Nothing about her situation was *light*. She hated him in that moment, hated him with a passion.

"That was not a Christmas kiss," she bit out, her eyes furiously stripping him of any further attempt at levity.

Any trace of a smile was wiped from his face. His

eyes suddenly gathered an intense focus, gleaming more yellow than gold. A wolf on the hunt, Amy thought wildly, determined on tracking through anything to get to her.

"No. It was much more," he quietly agreed.

Her heart squeezed into a tight ball. He was going to close in on her no matter what she said or did. She could feel the power of his purpose, and couldn't move away from it.

"Don't you find that curious, Amy?" he asked.

She had no answer. Her mind had seized up on the idea of his being an irresistible force.

"How well we get on now that Steve's out of the way?" he went on, the words seeming to beat at her in relentless pursuit. "How perfectly we click when we come together?"

Perfectly!

That triggered a rush of hysteria which was impossible to contain. The words bubbled out of her mind and spilled into irretrievable sound.

"Oh, so *perfectly* I'm pregnant, Jake!"

Her hands flew up in dramatic emphasis.

"How do you like that for perfect?"

CHAPTER SIXTEEN

SHOCK!

Amy saw it, felt it reverberating through Jake just as it quaked through her. It was like a live thing, with writhing tentacles, reaching and changing everything. She couldn't believe she'd done it...set this irrevocable happening in motion without any rational planning for consequences...just blurted it out...here it is...

"Pregnant."

The word fell from Jake's lips as though there was too much to take in and he couldn't quite cope with it.

Amy flapped her hands helplessly. "I'm sorry... I'm sorry... It was that night you came to my apartment and...and I forgot to take the pill after...after you'd gone. I took two the next day but..."

Her voice faltered as she saw the shock clear from Jake's face, to be replaced by a strange, wondrous look.

"You're pregnant to me," he said.

Amy didn't understand. He sounded as if he liked the idea. Maybe his thinking had been knocked haywire. "Jake..." It was of paramount importance to get through to him. "...It wasn't meant to happen..."

"But it did." He grinned from ear to ear.

Amy started to panic. His reaction wasn't right. He certainly wasn't thinking straight. "Are you listening to me?" she cried.

"You're carrying my child...mine!" He spoke as

though he'd won the best lottery in the world. "For a moment there, I thought it was Steve's, and that would have been hard, Amy. A hell of a reminder..."

"Jake, this is not okay!" she hurled at him, desperate to get the conversation on some kind of clear track. "It was an accident. I didn't want to hang it on you."

"Hang it on me! Hang it on me!" He repeated in a kind of dazed incredulity. "I'm the father. You're not hanging anything on me. The biological fact is..." He paused, apparently having been struck by a different thought. "How long have you known?"

"What?" Amy just couldn't get a handle on how Jake's mind was working. It was totally incomprehensible to her.

"About the baby."

"Oh!" She flushed. "I got the results of the blood test two days ago."

He grinned again. "So it *is* absolutely certain."

"Will you stop that?" she cried in exasperation.

"Stop what?"

"Looking so damned pleased about it!"

"I can't help it. It's not every day a man gets told he's going to be a father. We're talking about our first child..."

"Jake! We're...not...married," she almost shouted at him.

"Well, we can soon fix that," he said, his delighted expression moving swiftly to purpose.

Amy glared at him in helpless frustration. The man did not have his feet on the ground at all. Maybe he was besotted with the idea of being presented with a child of his own, having been surrounded by his siblings' children all day. Whatever the reason, there was no sense coming from him. He probably needed a few days to think about it, do some sober reflection on their situation.

"I'm going home," she stated firmly. "I've got a headache."

As she started to step past him his arm shot out to prevent it.

"Wait! Please..."

It was too much. Tears welled into her eyes. She was too choked up to speak, too distressed to look at him.

"I'm sorry. I'm not getting this right, am I?" he said softly, apologetically.

She shook her head.

"Don't cry, Amy. I'll do better, I promise."

The tears flowed faster.

Then his arm was around her shoulders, hugging her close for comfort. "I'll take you home."

She swallowed hard, struggling to get control of her voice. "Your family..."

"You're my family now, Amy. Let me at least take care of you."

That did it, speaking to her so gently, saying what she'd been secretly craving to hear. The tears were unstoppable now and he was already urging her to the front door, opening it for her. She didn't have the strength to fight him, didn't have voice enough to argue. They were out of the house and walking down the path to the street before he spoke again, his sympathetic tone soothing some of the turmoil inside her.

"It must have been rough on you the past two days, worrying about what to do."

"Yes," she managed to whisper.

"You're not…umh…thinking of a termination, are you, Amy?"

"No."

"Good!" His sigh expressed deep relief. "I'm not sure I could have borne that, either."

This was muttered more to himself than to her and Amy briefly puzzled over it. She was the one who had to do the bearing. Jake seemed to be off on another plane again. Though it was clear he wanted her to have the baby. He hadn't left her in any doubt about that. Though she had a mountain of doubts surrounding what would eventuate from it.

"The car key?" he prompted.

They'd reached the sidewalk where her car was parked at the kerb. She fumbled in her handbag and found the key, found a tissue, too, and wiped her weepy eyes. She was feeling slightly more in control, though still very shaky on how to proceed from here with Jake.

He held out his hand. "Better let me drive, Amy. I don't think you're in a fit enough state to concentrate on it."

Taking care of her…being kind. Jake *was* kind. For a moment Amy wallowed in the warm reassurance. He wasn't going to make this hard for her. He was prepared—more than prepared—to take responsibility. Which reminded her of other more immediate responsibilities.

"What about you? The champagne?" she asked, unsure how many glasses he'd consumed over lunch. The last thing she needed was to end up today in a police station with Jake charged for drunk driving.

"No problem." He gave her his quirky smile. "Sober as a judge."

Somehow that typical little smile put things on a more normal footing. She sighed, trying to loosen the tightness in her chest, and handed over the key, relieved he could take care of the driving, relieved also that he appeared to be more himself now.

Despite her headache, Amy decided it would be good to get a few things settled so she had some idea where she stood with him. And with her job. There was no longer any escape from the truth, so the sooner they talked it over, the better.

Jake unlocked the car, saw her settled in the passenger seat, then moved quickly to the driver's side, sliding in behind the wheel and closing them in together. *Together* was the operative word, she thought ruefully. They'd made this baby together and now they were stuck together until something was sorted out.

"One thing I want to say, Amy, before you do any more thinking."

She could feel him looking at her with urgent intensity but she couldn't bring herself to let him see just how vulnerable she was to whatever he had to say. It was easier to stare straight ahead, easier for steeling herself to face the difficulties he would certainly bring up.

"Go on," she invited, hoping she could cope with the outcome.

"Don't rule marriage out," he said quietly. "I want to marry you, Amy. I think we could have a good life together. So please give it your serious consideration while I drive you home."

He didn't wait for a reply, which was just as well,

because Amy was too poleaxed to speak. He switched on the engine and got on with driving.

She didn't really notice the journey home, wasn't aware of time passing. Her mind was in a ferment. How could she give marriage to Jake Carter serious consideration? What was he thinking of? It was time to take a wife and have a family and she'd do as well as anyone else, especially since she was already pregnant to him? The good old chemistry spark was there so why not?

Never mind that the spark might go out before she even had the baby! There was always a host of other available women to have on the side when that happened. Did he think he could fool her when she knew so much about him? It was true they got on well together, but how long would that last under pressures they'd never had before? She could not live with infidelity for a start!

It was all very well for his mother to say it wasn't in Jake's nature to cheat. Without love, they'd be cheating each other anyway if they got married. Besides, Elizabeth Rose Carter certainly wouldn't welcome her as a daughter-in-law. Though Jake could probably charm his mother into accepting anything if he worked at it.

Amy was only too aware of how charming he could be. She couldn't let it work on her. There was too much at stake here. Her happiness. Their child's happiness.

Their child...

Misery swamped her. It wasn't right to bring a child into the world when neither parent had planned for it. What was she to do? What did she want Jake to do?

Dazedly, she looked around for landmarks and realised they were heading down the hill to Balmoral Beach.

It reminded her of the day Jake first drove her here, the day she'd told him Steve was going to marry his pregnant blonde.

Pregnancy…marriage.

Did all men think like that?

No, of course they didn't. If men were so committed to their children there wouldn't be so many single mothers. Not that she wanted to be a single mother. That would be a very hard road. But getting married because of a baby…the thought of an oppressive prison loomed darkly on the edges of what looked like an easier road. Becoming dependent on a man who didn't really want to spend his life with her…

We could have a good life together.

Amy rubbed at her temples.

Did Jake really believe that?

"Headache worse?" he asked in concern.

"No. Just trying to think."

"Leave it until we get home," he advised. "Almost there."

It wasn't his home, Amy thought crossly. He was going to invade it again, as he had before…invading her life…but they did have to talk. He was the father of her child and there was no locking him out of their future. One way or another, he would always be in it. Especially if he kept up his current attitude.

He parked the car in her garage slot underneath the apartment block. She vaguely wondered how he knew which slot was hers. Probably a lucky guess.

As they rode up to the top floor in the elevator, Amy became acutely aware of Jake's physical nearness. She started remembering the kiss underneath the mistletoe and how she'd clung to him…how he'd felt, how much he could make her feel, the sheer power of his sexuality drawing on hers. If he started that again…tried to use it…she must not let him.

He held out her car key. She snatched it off his palm, frightened of any skin-to-skin contact with him. For a moment Jake's palm hung there empty and her graceless behaviour shot a wave of heat up Amy's throat.

Thankfully Jake made no comment. He lowered his hand to his side and Amy busied herself with her handbag, putting away the car key and finding the one for her front door.

Her inner tension increased, screaming along every nerve in her body as Jake accompanied her out of the elevator. Fortunately he had the good sense not to touch her. She would have snapped.

Once the door was unlocked, Jake gestured for her to precede him into the apartment, so she went ahead and left him to follow, grateful he was tactful enough not to crowd her and she had the chance to establish a comfortable distance. Having dropped her handbag on the kitchen counter, she walked straight across the living room to open the doors to the balcony.

The instant waft of fresh sea air on her hot face felt good. Unbelievably, despite her fevered thoughts, her headache had eased. If she could just keep enough cool to handle Jake in a calm and reasonable manner, maybe they could come to some workable agreements.

"Can I get you something, Amy? A cup of tea or…"

"No."

His voice came from the kitchen area. He'd probably paused there, watching her. She took a deep breath and turned to face him, forcing an ironic smile to ease the concern he was expressing. He was behind the counter, hands resting on it, poised to minister to her needs, but he was no more relaxed than she was.

His shoulders looked bunched, his facial muscles were taut, a worry line creased the space between his brows, his triangular eyes were narrowed, sharply scanning, weighing up her body language.

"Thank you," she added belatedly, "but I doubt anything would sit well in my stomach right now. I wasn't ready for this, Jake. Telling you, I mean."

He nodded. "Better done than churning about it, Amy."

"Yes. Though I didn't mean to mess up your Christmas day with your family. I only went to see…" She trailed off, finding it too difficult to describe all the nuances of her observations.

"What it might be like if you joined it?"

His quick perception jolted her. "I can't marry you," she blurted out more baldly than she had meant to.

He frowned. "Because of my family?"

"No…no…" She shook her head, berating herself for being as tactless as his mother. "You have a great family. It must be wonderful to belong to them. For you, I mean. For them. All of you…"

Now she was blathering. She stopped and took another deep breath. Her heart was fluttering. She couldn't seem to keep two coherent thoughts in her head.

"There's no reason why you couldn't belong, Amy," Jake said with serious intent. "And our child certainly would, as naturally as all the other children. You met

Tess and Grace and Martin today. You must have seen how they..."

"Please..." She waved an emphatic dismissal. "That's not the point, Jake."

"What is the point?"

"I wouldn't be living with them day in and day out. I'd be living with *you*."

"So?"

Living with anyone wasn't simple. Amy knew from living with Steve...the adjustments, the compromises. It was hard enough *with love*. Without it...and always worrying about Jake connecting with other women, beautiful women running after him all the time...

She shook her head. "I can't do it."

"Why not?"

The need for this torment to be ended formed her answer. She looked at him squarely, defying any further persistance on this question, sure there was no way of refuting what was necessary to her.

"I don't love you, Jake."

He stiffened. A muscle in his cheek contracted. It was as though she'd hit him physically and Amy had the strangest feeling—a strong, unshakable feeling—that she'd hurt him. Hurt him badly. Which rattled her. She hadn't considered Jake would be hurt by her rejection. Frustrated at not getting his own way, but not hurt.

She stared at him in wretched confusion and was caught by the changing expression in his eyes, the sharpening of his focus on her, the gathering of an intensity that felt like a powerful concentration of his will and energy, burning a challenge straight into her brain...a challenge that denied the knowledge she thought she had of him, denied even her knowledge of herself.

For a few riveting moments he seemed like a total stranger to her...or he took on dimensions she had not been aware of before. It gave her the scary feeling she was dealing with much more than she had anticipated, and she was suddenly riven with uncertainties. She almost jumped when he spoke.

"There is such a thing as a marriage of convenience, Amy. I believe it could work very well," he said quietly.

One certainty instantly exploded from all the thinking she'd done and because he'd unsettled her so deeply, she answered with fierce emphasis. "I will not be a *convenient* wife to you. That might suit you, Jake, out and about your life, but I don't see myself as the little woman at home, subservient to your needs."

"Subservient! Since when haven't I considered your needs?" His tone was harsher, edged with angry disbelief. "I've spent most of my time with you, putting your needs above my own. Can we have a bit of fair-mindedness here, Amy?"

She flushed, unable to pluck out one pertinent example of inconsideration on his part, and he'd been especially sensitive to her needs since Steve had dumped her. The long shadow of her parents' marriage crossed her mind...her mother serving her tyrannical father like a slave...but there was nothing tyrannical about Jake. He was more like a free-wheeling buccaneer, happy to lead anyone into adventurous fun.

"I want a marriage of sharing, Amy," he pressed. "We happen to do that well."

"Am I supposed to share you with all the women you

fancy?'' she flared, fighting her way out of being in the wrong.

"That's enough!''

He slammed his hand down on the counter, the angry frustration he'd repressed erupting with such force, Amy shrank back against the door. Then was angry at herself for being intimidated.

"Don't like the truth, Jake?'' she challenged, her chin lifting into fighting mode.

"You want the truth?'' he flung back at her, too incensed to back down this time. "I'll give it to you. The high turnover of women in my life can be placed entirely at your door.''

"Mine?'' she retorted incredulously.

"Yours!'' He stabbed a finger at her. "So try swallowing that for a change instead of spitting out slurs on my lack of staying power.''

"And just *how* can it be my fault?''

"Because what we sparked off each other—and don't you deny it, Amy—was stronger than anything I felt with the women I tried to relate to. Tried, because you made yourself inaccessible to me and it seemed pointless to wait for something that might never happen.''

The sheer passion in his voice rocked her into silence.

His eyes flashed with savage mockery. "Oh, you did your best to block it out...the natural connection that was always there between us. With two long years of blocking it out, it's become a habit, hasn't it? Keep Jake at a distance. Don't let him close because something big might slip out of your control.''

A fierce pride hardened his features. "Which it did.

The night we made a baby was bigger than anything I've felt in my life. And I'll bet my life it was for you, too."

His mouth twisted into a bitter grimace. "Two years wasted while I was fool enough to respect your commitment to a guy who ended up cheating on you. Two years...and now you want to waste the lot, clinging to some prejudicial rubbish."

His eyes glittered derision at her. "Give her more time, I told myself. She's still getting over that bastard. You'll win her in the end, Jake."

He shook his head. "You're not even prepared to give me a chance for the sake of our child."

The indictment he was delivering was so devastating, Amy could do nothing but listen, absorbing shock after shock as he forced her to recognise and acknowledge a different perception from what she had allowed herself. And the worst of it was, there was ample evidence to back up all he was saying.

She *had* used Steve as a barrier between them, no denying it if she was truly honest.

Once the barrier was gone...

She remembered Jake rattling on to baby Joshua after he'd learnt Steve was out of her life... *We've got Amy Taylor right where we want her...well, not precisely.*

Then later when she'd said she was on her own, Jake reminding her...*I was here for you. When your scumbag of a lover let you down, I was here for you.*

You do have me to count on.

Ruth's attitude to her...the Wonderwoman in Jake's life ever since she'd begun working for him. Even his mother saying Jake had talked so much about her... And they'd all told her she was the only woman he'd ever wanted to share his family Christmas.

The night of their *mating* flooded back into her mind... Jake asking her not to forget it, a special memory...uniquely special...and it truly had been...but she'd twisted it all to fit a different picture to the real truth...the truth he'd just forced her to see...the truth that damned everything she'd said and thought.

She saw the anger drain out of him, saw the passion give way to sadness, and had the sinking feeling she had dug her own grave and there was no way out of it.

"One day you'll have to explain to our child why you wouldn't marry me," he put to her, his eyes dull and opaque, blocking her out of his heart. "If you have to keep lying to yourself...well, I guess that's your choice. But don't lie to my child about me, Amy. I don't deserve that."

Her heart felt like stone. She had done him so many terrible injustices. And for what? To ensure she was protected against her own natural impulses, her own instincts? Jake was twice the man Steve was. More. She'd always known it. Of course she had. And told herself he was too much to handle, too risky to take on. He was too handsome, too attractive, and there was too much competition for him. She wasn't good enough to hold him.

Not good enough...

It was what her father had always said to her.

So she'd stayed with less, chosen safety, and told herself it was sensible, right, for the best.

Jake stepped back from the counter, stood very straight and tall, a man who'd fought and lost but not without dignity, not without courage and fire and belief in himself.

"Ask whatever you want of me and I'll give it to you," he said flatly. "But let's leave it for a few days. When you come back to work will be soon enough. I'll listen to your plans then. I've lost any taste for them right now."

He nodded to her. "If you'll excuse me…"

Without waiting for a reply, not expecting one, he moved out of the kitchen and headed for the front door. For several seconds, Amy was completely paralysed. The click of the knob being turned snapped her out of it.

"Wait!" Her voice was little more than a hoarse croak. She rushed to the far edge of the kitchen counter, desperately calling, "Jake, please wait!"

He stood at the end of the short hall, his back turned to her, his hand still on the doorknob, his shoulders squared, but his head was thrown high as though in acute listening mode.

He *was* waiting. Not inviting any more from her, but prepared to hear why she wanted to stop him from going. If she didn't get it right, he would go. She knew he would.

"What is it?" he rasped, impatient with her silence.

What could she say? Amy only knew she had to stop him from walking out of her life. Then the words came, sure and true.

"I'll marry you. I will. If you'll still have me."

CHAPTER SEVENTEEN

TENSION racked Amy as she watched Jake's shoulders rise and fall. It had to be a deep, deep breath he was taking and she had no idea what emotion he might be fighting to control.

Then he turned.

Slowly.

Amy *held* her breath.

He looked at her as though he didn't know her, scanning for a recognition which should have been there, but had somehow slipped past him. "Why, Amy?"

"Because..." The grave she'd dug for herself was so huge, so deep, she quailed at the task of climbing out of it. Her stomach contracted in sheer panic. Her mind skittered all over the place, finally grasping a hook Jake had given her. "What you said is true. I've lied and lied and lied, to stop myself...to stop *you* from getting too close to me."

His face tightened. His eyes gleamed yellow, hard and merciless. "That hardly makes marriage desirable for either of us," he bit out derisively.

Her hands fluttered out in desperate appeal. "I don't know how to explain it to you."

"Try!" It was a harsh, gutteral sound, scraped from wounds too freshly delivered for him to accept any evasion from her.

Amy knew it was a demand she had to meet, yet

165

where to start, how to make him understand? She hadn't understood it herself until he'd started putting it together for her.

"No backward steps now, Amy," he warned.

"You once asked me about my family," she plunged in, her eyes begging his forebearance. "I glossed over it, Jake."

Impatience exploded from him, his hands cutting the air in a sharp-scissor motion. "What can your family possibly have to do with us? You told me they've been out of your life for years."

"Control," she answered quickly, frantic to capture his attention and keep it. "With your upbringing, you couldn't imagine what my childhood was like...the constant emotional abuse from my father...having to wear it...trying not to be crushed. When I left home at sixteen, I swore never to let anyone have control over me again...not...not in an emotional sense."

"You expect me to accept that? After all the emotion you spent on your ex-lover?" he hurled at her in disgust. "Was it five years of nothing? Is that what you're telling me?"

"It wasn't like that!" she cried.

"You're not making sense to me, Amy."

"With Steve...there was never any talk of marriage between us. He called us *free spirits*. I felt...*safe*...with him."

"Safe!" Jake jeered.

"Yes, *safe!*" she snapped. "If you don't want to hear this, just go," she hurled back at him, driven to the end of her tether.

"Oh, I wouldn't miss this story for anything," he retorted scathingly. "Do go on."

Amy paused, taking a deep breath to calm herself. Her heart was thundering. The pulse in her temples was throbbing. There was no escape from this pain. It had to be faced, dealt with. Then the choice of what to do would be Jake's.

"If you want to understand anything about me instead of leaping to your own coloured judgements, then you'll listen," she told him as forcefully as she could. "If only for the sake of your child, you should listen."

The mention of the baby visibly pulled him back from the more personal issues between them. He took on an icy demeanour. "I'm listening."

They were so cold those words, Amy shivered. Nevertheless, she stuck grimly to her course, determined now to lay out the truth, whatever the consequences.

"To get back to Steve. He came from a damaged family, too. It effects people, Jake. You want someone—no one likes being alone—but you don't want to be owned. Because that's threatening."

He frowned, assessing what she was saying.

Encouraged, Amy rushed on to the vital point. "You threatened my sense of safety, Jake."

It startled him. He cocked his head on one side, considering this new perspective, his eyes still reserved but intensely watchful.

"You had the power to get at me, no matter how guarded I was against it. I guess you could say Steve was my bolthole from you."

Another jerk of his head, seemingly negative to Amy's view.

"Call me a coward if you like," she offered, feeling a heavy load of self-contempt for all the running away she'd done. "I *was* a coward with you."

"No." His eyes flashed hard certainty. "You always stood up to me."

"That wasn't brave. It was the only way to retain control," she pressed, trying to reach him on what she saw as the crux of everything. "I lost it the night you came here. I didn't listen to what you were saying afterwards. I was fighting to regain *control,* fighting your power to..." She paused, trying to get it right for him. "...To take over my life and do whatever you wanted with me."

He shook his head, patently appalled at how she had thought. "Amy, you'd always have a say in it. I've respected your wishes. I'd never not respect them," he argued, fiercely dismissing what probably seemed to him a gross allegation.

"I realise that now," she acknowledged. "But I was too frightened to see it then. I kept pushing you away from me, trying to protect myself. I tried to cling to the idea of *spontaneous combustion*. It was like an excuse. But you said it more truly a few minutes ago... *something big slipping out of control.*"

"But our child..." he burst out in angry confusion. "Didn't the baby we made...and its future...deserve some re-thinking?"

"I've been frightened of that, too, pushing it away from me," she confessed.

"But you want the baby. You said...you assured me..."

"That I wasn't thinking of a termination," she finished for him, leaping ahead, anxious to get it all out now. "I couldn't, Jake. Not because it was my baby. This will probably sound unreal to you, but from the moment the pregnancy was confirmed, I thought of the baby as *yours*."

"Blaming me?"

"No...no..." She shook her head vehemently, anguished by his misunderstanding. "I meant...you have this power, Jake. It...it clouds everything. I didn't think of it as *my* baby. Not even an entity by itself. It was like a bond you'd made with me. A tie. And I see-sawed between wanting the link with you and being frightened of what it might mean to me."

"Frightened... you're *frightened* of marrying me?" He looked repelled by the idea.

"I was. I'm not anymore," she cried in a fluster. "Don't you see?" she pleaded. "There was no way out because of the baby. And if you hurt me...it's like a trap. I can't bring myself to let you go...yet you have the power to damage me far more than my father ever did. For far longer."

"You have the same power over me," he said tersely. "Don't you realise that?"

It jolted her. She hadn't realised it. Hadn't even thought of it. Yet she'd seen the hurt she'd given him, was watching the pain of her rejection working through him now as she pleaded her case.

"The power goes both ways," he said less harshly. "It's up to both of us not to abuse it."

She rubbed at her forehead. "I don't know what to do. The baby..." She looked down at her stomach, touched it tentatively. "It's still unreal to me as mine.

Maybe I'm not maternal. I wanted it to belong to your family. I don't think I know how to be a mother. My own mother…'' She raised anguished eyes. ''…She was too frightened of my father to stand up for us.''

''It only takes love, Amy. Freely given.'' He grimaced. ''Maybe your mother didn't feel free to give it. But there's no reason you can't. At least to our child.''

Freely given…he'd said that to her before…the night they'd made the baby…their baby. She wished she could feel good about it, that it wasn't some kind of a trap for either of them. Maybe that would come. She hoped so. She needed to feel good. Good enough, anyway.

Jake still didn't know all he had to know, and she had to tell him. No more lies. No evasions. Her eyes ached with the need to reach him as she said, ''I do want you, Jake. I've wanted you for so long… I said I didn't want to go to bed with you but that was another lie. I lied because I didn't want you to know how much I had thought about it, how much I wanted it. Wanted you…''

She could read no reaction from him. He was completely still. Whether he was absorbing what she said or shutting it out she couldn't tell. She felt drained from the effort of unburdening herself to him, yet the compulsion to draw him back to her would not let her rest.

''Today, when you kissed me under the mistletoe… I wanted to believe what you made me feel was forever. It meant…too much. It scared me again. And then you said…it was only a Christmas kiss…''

''No,'' he denied vehemently. ''I said a man was entitled to kiss a woman standing under a mistletoe on Christmas day.''

"So I screwed that up, too," she said helplessly. "I guess I've made it too hard for you to believe me now."

"What's too hard for me to believe, Amy?"

Not too hard. Impossible. But she said it anyway.

"I love you, Jake."

It was true. She loved everything about him, loved him so much it hurt. Her heart was bleeding with all she felt for him. And it hurt all the more because he hadn't said he loved her. He wasn't saying it now, either. He just stood there, staring at her with seemingly unseeing eyes.

Maybe he didn't love her and was shocked by her confession. She'd assumed...but it could have been his ego hurt by her blanket rejection, not his heart. Why hadn't she thought of that? Because she needed... Dear God! She *needed* his love. *She couldn't marry him without it.*

"Jake..." His name scraped out of her convulsing throat. She swallowed hard. Her hands lifted in agitated appeal. "...If you don't love me..."

He moved then. Before Amy could take a breath she was wrapped in his arms and held so close she could feel his heart beating and his warmth flooding through her. She wrapped her own arms around his neck, buried her face against his broad shoulder, and hung on for dear life as tremors racked her body and her mind slipped into meltdown, knowing only that Jake had taken her back, he was holding her safe, and they were together again.

He rubbed his cheek against her hair, tenderly soothing. "Don't be frightened of me. Not ever, Amy," he said, his voice furred with passionate feeling. "If you'll just open your heart to me, I'll listen. We'll work things out together. That's how it should be.''

He'd forgiven her. The relief of it went through her like a tidal wave.

"Maybe I should have spoken...instead of holding back," he went on, his own torment pouring out. "I guess we all try to protect ourselves from hurt. You'd been with Steve for so long... I was wary of a rebound effect. I wanted you free and clear of him, Amy, before I told you how I felt."

How could she blame him? She'd given him so little to work on.

He sighed, his warm breath caressing her ear. "I've loved you for a very long time. I can't imagine not loving you."

He loved her.

It wasn't just for the baby.

It wasn't only the pull of physical chemistry.

He loved her.

The wonderful surge of energy that shot through Amy pushed her head up. She wanted—needed—to see. There was no mistake this time. No misreading. The molten gold in his eyes glowed with such rich depth of feeling, she knew instinctively this was only the tip of a river that flowed through every part of him.

"But I do need some love back from you without having to fight for it," he pleaded, searching her eyes for it. "Do you understand?"

"Freely given," she whispered, awed by the strength of his giving.

"Yes."

She didn't hesitate. She went up on tiptoe, pulled his

head down to hers and kissed him with all the passion his giving had released. A storm of passion. Years of pent-up feeling, freed at last, to be expressed, revelled in with joy and love and the deepest, most intense pleasure. No fear. Not the tiniest hint of fear or worry or doubt about anything. He loved her. She loved him. And the baby made a beautiful bond between them.

She took him to bed with her, showing him it was her choice, her desire, her wish to share everything with him, openly and honestly, and they made love for a very long time. There was no need to stop and every need to experience and learn all they wanted to learn of each other. The wonder of touching—touching without any inhibitions—was incredibly marvellous.

Jake was the most magnificent man. In every way. She adored him. And he adored her right back…sensually, sexually, emotionally. And when he kissed and caressed her stomach so lovingly, and she saw the happiness and pleasure in his eyes at the thought of her carrying his baby inside—their baby—she suddenly felt an intense wave of love for the life they had created, Jake and her together…their child…who would be brought up with love…freely given.

Instead of being dark and fearful and threatening, the future now shone with so much glorious promise.

Except…

"Jake!" In a rush of agitation, she lifted his head up.

"Mmh…" He smiled at her, his eyes dancing with teasing wickedness. "Can't I do what I want with you now?"

"Yes, but…" She sighed. "Your mother doesn't like me, Jake. She won't approve of us marrying."

"Ah!" He sobered into serious speculation. "I suspected something had gone on between you today. So what did?"

Amy grimaced at the unpleasant memory. "Your mother thinks I'm loose...living with Steve...not marrying him. She said my mother would have advised me it wasn't good. Wasn't right."

"She spoke out of ignorance, Amy," he said soothingly. "That can easily be fixed."

"It was like she was warning me off you, Jake."

"No." He gave his quirky smile. "Just warning you off living with me. She got upset about me giving you the apartment."

"What?"

"Okay..." He rolled his eyes. "I've been a bit devious, but it was for your own good, Amy."

"This is your apartment?" she squeaked. The colours used in the decor...his knowledge of her garage...

"I just wanted you away from any memory of Steve, so I fixed it with Ted Durkin and..."

"You made up all those conditions?"

"Well, the rent was too steep so I had to bring it down in a way you'd accept."

"And Ted Durkin was in on it?" She remembered her suspicion at the time, the suspicion she'd dismissed because of Ted Durkin's manner.

"He helped me make up a credible cover story."

"Oh!" She didn't know whether to feel outraged or...beautifully taken care of.

"Anyhow, Mum thought I was plotting to set you up as my mistress. But I wasn't, Amy. I truly wasn't. Marriage was always on my mind."

She laughed, suddenly remembering something else. "You just wanted to get me where you wanted me." Her eyes danced back at his.

"Precisely," he agreed, completely unabashed.

And she laughed some more, all the doubts of the past behind her.

"Mum probably thought, because you'd lived with Steve, you might choose to do that with me, too, so she was trying to steer you straight." He heaved an exasperated sigh. "She just can't keep out of things."

Amy sobered up. "I'm afraid I said some harsh things to her, Jake. About you and your women. Sorry, but..." She shook her head regretfully. "I was really quite rude, cutting her off when she tried to defend you."

He shrugged. "All's well that ends well, Amy. I'll call her now, fix it up."

His confidence amazed her. He leaned over, picked up the bedside telephone, dialed, listened, then said, "It's Jake, Ruth. Is Mum still there?"

He sighed as his sister apparently rattled on.

"Never mind that, get Mum for me." He smiled at Amy. "Ruth's all excited about seeing us kissing. She knows how I feel about you."

"Do they all?" Amy asked curiously.

"More or less. I'm no good at hiding things from my family," he confessed.

Then he'd be no good at hiding things from her anymore, either, Amy happily decided. Not that he was trying to. She thought fleetingly of Steve who'd clam up like an oyster whenever she'd tried to dig anything out of him. It was so different with Jake, ecstatically different.

"Mum?"

Apparently his mother rattled on to him, too. His family were certainly great talkers. Which was good. Great! Nothing repressed or suppressed.

"No, you haven't ruined everything." His eyes twinkled at Amy. "In fact, things couldn't be better. Amy loves me and she wants to marry me. Except she thinks you don't approve of her."

Another long speech which Jake interpreted for Amy as it went on.

"Mum is very sorry...she didn't mean to give that impression...she thinks you're beautiful...she thinks we're well suited...and you obviously have good sense and taste to choose me as your husband...she's relieved she didn't upset the applecart, so to speak...we're invited to lunch tomorrow...so she can show you how happy she is about us...is that okay, Amy?"

She nodded.

"We'll be there, Mum." He grinned as he put the receiver down. "She says this is the best Christmas ever. The last one of her brood finally settling down." He laughed, all his shadows gone, too. "It certainly is the best Christmas for me, Amy."

"Me, too," she agreed, her heart brimming over with happiness.

Jake gathered her close and kissed her, and she stretched against him languorously, provocatively, wanting all of him again. He was not slow to oblige, and Amy exulted in the sense of belonging to him, not Jake the rake, *her* Jake, always and forever.

And she'd belong to his wonderful family, too.

No more being alone.

Not for her nor her baby.

Their baby.

The miracle of love, she thought, and gave herself up to it.

Freely.

CHAPTER EIGHTEEN

NEW Year's Eve...

Amy watched *Free Spirit* gliding through the water to the wharf. It was a beautiful yacht, long sleek lines, exuding luxury, glamour, no expense spared in design or amenities. Murmurs of excitement and pleasurable anticipation ran around the select group of Jake's clients as they waited to board.

Free Spirit...

The name reminded her of Steve. And his blonde. Tonight was their wedding night. But she was not going to drown herself. No way. She was going to have a wonderful night with Jake, a wonderful life with him, too. In fact, she was more free with Jake than she'd ever felt before.

The men in the group wore formal dinner suits, adding style and class to the festive evening. Amy couldn't help feeling pride in the fact that not one of them looked as handsome as Jake. He outshone them all. The strange part was, she didn't feel the least bit insecure about it. Jake had only to glance at her and she knew no other woman here—regardless of beauty or finery—held a candle to her, not in Jake's mind.

She smiled to herself, remembering the women's magazine with the article on exit signs. It was still in the bottom drawer of her desk at the office, still unread. No need to read it now. Or ever. Jake believed implicitly in the marriage vows. Absolute commitment. For better, for worse...until death do us part.

Since Christmas, she had seen so much more of his family, and they all shared the same attitude. They'd been brought up to view a good marriage as the most desirable state in life, with children as the blessed bonus. Not one of them had anything negative to say when Jake had made the announcement about the baby. Expressions of delight, congratulations, offers of help from all the women were instantly forthcoming. And Jake's mother could not have been nicer, only too happy to push wedding plans.

Amy shook her head over her initial impression of Elizabeth Rose Carter. Jake's mother was really a very generous person, wanting everything to be lovely and possibly a little too concerned that it be so. His father had more of an optimistic, let-it-be outlook, confident his children would work out what was best for themselves. Amy considered him a real darling.

As the yacht docked and two of the deckhands started sliding out the boarding ramp, Jake hooked Amy's arm around his and smiled at her. "Ready to start hostessing?"

"Lead on." she replied happily.

His smile turned quirky. "Actually you don't have to hostess. I've hired people to do the necessary."

"But you said..."

"I needed some excuse to get you on this cruise with me." His eyes sparkled wickedly. "It was my seduction plan. And I see no reason to change it."

She laughed, hugging him closer to her as they walked to the ramp.

"You know, Amy, you look stunning in red but I've got to say, that blue you're wearing completely knocks me out." he declared decisively.

"You really like this outfit?" It was a long skirt and tunic in a soft, slinky, royal blue fabric, to which she'd added an ornate silver belt, silver shoes and silver jewellery.

His eyes gleamed gold. "You give it the magic of the night, my love."

"Mmh...keep up that seductive talk and who knows where it may get you?"

He laughed.

They were both of them bubbling with good humour as they preceded their party onto the yacht. A flight of steps led up to the main sundeck, an outdoor entertainment centre with a long bench lounge, table, chairs. Two hostesses hovered by a bar table which had been set up with wines, beer, fruit juice, iced water.

"Champagne, sir?" one of them instantly asked Jake, her eyes feasting on his every feature.

"Two, thank you." he replied, indicating Amy be served first.

Jake in control, and not the least bit interested in other women's interest, Amy observed. As he'd once said to her, any amount of interest was futile when it wasn't returned.

They moved to a position by the door leading in to the formal saloon, ready to greet everyone as they passed through to check out the luxurious appointments of the yacht.

In the saloon, three long deeply cushioned sofas, their cream upholstery trimmed with terracotta piping, were positioned around a polished granite coffee table, graced by an artistic floral arrangement. Beyond it was the formal dining room, its black lacquered table surrounded by black leather chairs.

Below, there were two queen-size staterooms with full ensuites and two twin bedrooms with ensuites, as well, all of the rooms designer decorated. The rear deck featured a spa-pool, and the bridge deck above them provided more lounging space for a topside view of their cruising around the harbour.

Amy was ready with all the facts and figures about the yacht should anyone ask. Mostly, the clients and their guests wanted to see for themselves, passing by her and Jake after a few words, happy to explore and assess everything on their own.

"Jake, darling!"

Amy glanced back from chatting to one couple to find the voluptuous blonde who'd fallen on Jake at *The Watermark,* coming on strongly again... Isabella Maddison...red talons raised ready to grab and dig in.

The sight of Amy stepping back to Jake's side stopped her in mid-pounce. The feline green eyes flashed venom.

"Oh! I see you have your companion with you."

"More than that, Isabella." Jake informed her, sliding his arm around Amy's shoulders and bestowing a smile lit with very possessive love on her. "My wife-to-be. Amy has finally agreed to marry me."

"Finally?" Isabella echoed in shock.

"Yes." Amy confirmed, ostentatiously holding up her left hand where Jake had placed a magnificent solitaire diamond ring on her third finger. She wriggled her fingers to make it flash under Isabella's catty eyes. "I decided to haul him in for good. It's time we had a family."

"Well…congratulations." came the weak rejoinder.

"Do help yourself to champagne." Amy invited sweetly. "This is a cruise to really enjoy."

"Yes…thank you."

Off she moved in a daze and Amy couldn't help grinning at Jake.

His wolf eyes gleamed. "You *were* jealous of her that day at *The Watermark*."

"I could have scratched her eyes out." Amy admitted.

"I should have raced you off to bed that afternoon."

"You can do it tonight instead."

"Oh, I will. I will." he promised her. "Though I doubt we'll make it as far as the bed."

Which put Amy in such a high state of sexual arousal, she barely tasted the gourmet food circulated by the hostesses; smoked salmon with a sprinkling of caviar, swordfish wrapped in Chinese spinach, little cups of sweet lamb curry and rice, deep-fried corn fritters, tandoori chicken kebabs. She tried them all, wanting to experience everything about tonight, but her awareness of Jake was uppermost.

It was a beautiful evening, a clear sky filling with stars as it darkened, only a light breeze ruffling the water, the warmth of the long summer day still lingering in the air.

The harbour was almost a maze of yachts, all sorts of small crafts, pleasure boats, the tall ships that had sailed in from around the world, ferries trying to weave through them all.

Crowds had gathered at vantage points around the foreshores, some of them virtually hanging on cliffs, clinging to rocks, waiting to see the fireworks display. It seemed as though all of Sydney had come out to watch the spectacle and celebrate New Year's Eve together.

The captain positioned *Free Spirit* mid-harbour, quite close to Fort Denison, giving a centre-stage view of the Opera House and the great Coat-hanger bridge which would be highly featured by the fireworks. As twilight sunk into the darkness of night, most of the guests moved up to the top deck, Jake and Amy with them. The display was scheduled to begin at nine o'clock, so families could enjoy it before children became too tired.

Amy leant against the waist-high railing. Jake stood behind her, his arms encircling her, holding her close, letting her feel his arousal, exciting her with it. There might have been only the two of them, alone together. Everyone was looking skywards, waiting for the darkness to light up with colour.

Then the fireworks began, shooting up from the great stone pylons that supported the bridge—huge explosive bursts of stars, balls of brilliant colour growing bigger and bigger before showering the sky with a brilliant rain of sparks, the whole skyline erupting in a wildly splendid mingling of reds and blues and greens and gold and silver. It was magical, glorious, totally captivating. It went on and on, becoming more and more surprising, stunning, fantastic. The whole span of the bridge came alight, streams of gold pouring down to the water far below it.

"What are you thinking?" Jake murmured in her ear.

"I was thinking of our wedding night and how it will feel." Amy whispered.

"How do you imagine it will feel?"

"Like this, Jake. Like this."

Suddenly, flashing across the huge coat hanger arch were the two curved lines of a smiling mouth, outlined in brilliant gold.

"Yes." Jake breathed in awe. "Just like that."

Amy's heart swelled with love and happiness and wonder.

A smile...

The smile of fulfilment...

On their wedding night.

If you enjoyed what you just read,
then we've got an offer you can't resist!

Take 2 bestselling love stories FREE!

Plus get a FREE surprise gift!

Rebellious, bold and...
a father!

THE AUSTRALIANS

Stories of romance Australian-style, guaranteed to
fulfill that sense of adventure!

This May 1999 look for

Taming a Husband

by **Elizabeth Duke**

Jake Thorn has never been one to settle down. He couldn't
stay with Lexie, even though his heart yearned to, and he
struck out across the continent before she could tell the
daddy-to-be the big news. Now, determined to give love
another chance, Jake has returned—and is shocked to find
himself a father!

*The Wonder from Down Under: where spirited women win
the hearts of Australia's most independent men!*

Available May 1999
at your favorite retail outlet.

HARLEQUIN®
Makes any time special ™

EXPECTING

She's sexy, she's successful... and she's pregnant!

Relax and enjoy these new stories about spirited women and gorgeous men, whose passion results in pregnancies... sometimes unexpectedly! All the new parents-to-be will discover that the business of making babies brings with it the most special love of all....

Harlequin Presents® brings you one **EXPECTING!** book each month throughout 1999.
Look out for:

The Unexpected Father by Kathryn Ross
Harlequin Presents® #2022, April 1999

The Playboy's Baby by Mary Lyons
Harlequin Presents® #2028, May 1999

Accidental Baby by Kim Lawrence
Harlequin Presents® #2034, June 1999

Available wherever Harlequin books are sold.

HARLEQUIN®
Makes any time special ™

Coming Next Month

HARLEQUIN PRESENTS®

THE BEST HAS JUST GOTTEN BETTER!

#2025 THE PERFECT LOVER Penny Jordan
(A Perfect Family)
While recovering from the emotional blow of unrequited love, Louise Crighton had rebounded into Gareth Simmonds's passionate arms. They'd shared a whirlwind holiday romance... but now their paths were about to cross again....

#2026 THE MILLIONAIRE'S MISTRESS Miranda Lee
(Presents Passion)
When Justine waltzed into Marcus's office, making it clear she'd do *anything* for a loan, he assumed she was just a gold-digger. He still desired her though, and she became his mistress. Then he realized how wrong he'd been....

#2027 MARRIAGE ON THE EDGE Sandra Marton
(The Barons)
Gage Baron's wife, Natalie, had just left him, and the last thing he wanted to do was go to his father's birthday party. But it was an opportunity to win back his wife; his father expected Natalie to attend the party and share Gage's bed!

#2028 THE PLAYBOY'S BABY Mary Lyons
(Expecting!)
As a successful career girl, Samantha thought she could handle a no-strings relationship with her old flame, Matthew Warner. But Sam had broken both the rules: she'd fallen in love with the sexy playboy *and* fallen pregnant!

#2029 GIORDANNI'S PROPOSAL Jacqueline Baird
Beth suspected that Italian tycoon Dex Giordanni had only asked her to marry him to settle a family score. She broke off the engagement, but Dex wasn't taking no for an answer; if she wasn't his fiancée, she'd have to be his mistress!

#2030 THE SEDUCTION GAME Sara Craven
Tara Lyndon had almost given up on men until she met gorgeous hunk Adam Barnard. Unfortunately, this perfect man also had a "perfect fiancée" waiting in the wings. There was only one thing to do to get her man: seduce him!